He was halfway down the street when someone suddenly stepped out of a doorway from his right. The blow was too swift for him to react to properly, but his natural reflexes enabled him to avoid its full force. As it was, it struck him on the point of the right shoulder, effectively paralyzing his right arm and hand.

He didn't know exactly what he'd been hit with, but he knew that it hurt like hell, and that he wouldn't be able to use his right arm to defend himself—or draw his gun.

Don't miss any of the lusty, hard-riding action in the Charter Western series, THE GUNSMITH

And coming next month:

THE GUNSMITH

36

BLACK PEARL SALOON

J.R. ROBERTS

CHARTER BOOKS, NEW YORK

THE GUNSMITH #36: BLACK PEARL SALOON

A Charter Book/published by arrangement with
the author

PRINTING HISTORY
Charter Original/January 1985

ISBN: 0-441-30915-1

Charter Books are published by The Berkley Publishing Group,
200 Madison Avenue, New York, New York 10016.
PRINTED IN THE UNITED STATES OF AMERICA

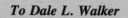

To Dale L. Walker

ONE

The last person Clint Adams would have expected to receive a telegram from in Wattsburgh, Arizona Territory was Dan Chow. He *had* ridden with a little Oriental—and the black man, Fred Hammer,* but would not have called either man his friend, nor would he have ever expected to hear from either one again—especially asking for a favor.

Clint was having breakfast with a lady named Delilah Ward in his hotel room when there was a knock on the door.

"Don't you dare!" Delilah said, grabbing him by the naked buttocks. His rigid manhood was buried to the hilt inside her slick love tunnel, and the last thing either one of them wanted to do at that moment was break the contact.

"The door," he said, gasping as her long nails bit into his flesh.

"They can wait."

A heavy fist began to beat on the door again.

"Who is it?" Clint shouted.

"Telegram."

"Jesus," Clint said as Delilah wrapped her long, powerful legs around his waist, sucking him even deeper inside of her.

* The Gunsmith #31: Trouble Rides a Fast Horse

"Telegram!" the impatient voice said from the hallway again.

"Slide it under the door, damn it!" Delilah shouted.

"He's worried about his tip," Clint said.

"Let him go to hell and get it!" she said fiercely, and suddenly they were coming together and everything else was forgotten.

Afterward Clint got out of bed and retrieved the telegram from the floor.

"I hope it's important," Delilah said from the bed. He looked over at her and once again admired the long, slim lines of her body and her full, firm breasts which were too big for the rest of her. If it weren't for those lovely, large mounds of rust-tipped flesh she'd be a tall, skinny woman with an insatiable appetite for sex. Her breasts were just the icing on an already tasty cake.

"It would have to be to take me away from you."

She smiled at him and said, "Sweet man."

Clint read the telegram, which had been forwarded from Labyrinth, Texas, and was surprised first, because it was from Dan Chow and second, because the little Oriental was asking him for a favor.

In essence, the telegram was asking Clint to go to San Francisco to a saloon called the Black Pearl Saloon, on the Barbary Coast, where he would meet Dan Chow's sister, Su. Clint was surprised also because Dan Chow had chosen a saloon that he knew of in San Francisco, although he was sure that the Oriental was unaware of that. There was a date for the meeting as well, which gave Clint ample travel time, if he were so inclined.

"Important?" Delilah asked.

"More like puzzling," he said. Why would Dan

Chow think he would respond to such a message? Was it simply because they had ridden together? It couldn't be because the Oriental had saved his life—he had, but they had done the same for each other several times over during that time. Neither man owed the other anything in Clint's eyes, but then Orientals tended to see things differently.

"What's it about?" Delilah asked with obvious curiosity. Suddenly Clint thought he knew that was what Dan Chow was depending on.

Curiosity.

Clint put the telegram aside and walked back to the bed, intent on forgetting it.

"It's not more important than what I have in mind," he said, sitting next to her and running his hands over her big breasts. "How did such a skinny girl get such big breasts?" he asked, tweaking her nipples playfully. But in spite of himself—and Delilah's obvious charms—he found himself unable to forget the telegram from Dan Chow.

Delilah and Clint were saying good-bye, as Delilah was leaving Wattsburgh that afternoon. After she was gone, the town would lose its appeal for Clint, and he had every intention of leaving himself—but he hadn't told her that. She would have suggested that he go the same way she was, and he didn't want that. She was a lovely distraction for the time he was in Wattsburgh, but nothing more.

After he saw her off at the stage, Clint went to the Wattsburgh Saloon, got himself a beer and sat at a corner table to try and decide which way to go next. He was acutely aware of the telegram from Dan Chow burning a hole in his shirt pocket.

He took it out, put it on the table, and smoothed it out. He read it again and admitted to himself that his curiosity was getting the better of him. Dan Chow had spoken briefly about his sister, Su Chow, and Clint had been curious about her even then.

Well, he wasn't doing anything at the present time but drifting, so he might as well drift his way toward San Francisco. At the very least he could visit a couple of friends, private detectives named John Chang and Sam Wing, whom he had met the last time he was in that city.*

Sure Adams, he thought, tucking the telegram back into his pocket, who do you think you're kidding?

* The Gunsmith #27: Chinatown Hell

TWO

Clint could have left his rig to be cared for in Wattsburgh and simply ridden Duke to San Francisco. It certainly would have made for a shorter trip. By taking the wagon, however, he was proving to some unseen force that he really was not *trying* to make the date set for the meeting at the Black Pearl Saloon.

In spite of the limitations imposed by the rig, he made San Francisco the day before the date on the telegram. Since he knew where the meeting place was, he put the rig, team, and Duke up at the same livery he had used his last trip, on Post Street.

If San Francisco had changed it had become larger and busier. Market Street and Kearny Street impressed the Gunsmith all over again, with their four-and-five-story buildings and expensive stores and shops.

The liveryman was not the same one who had been there before, but his reaction was the same as that of his predecessor: he was tremendously impressed with the stature of Duke and promised to take special care of the big black gelding.

Clint would have checked into one of the large, expensive hotels in San Francisco's Portsmouth Square, had he been in town simply to enjoy its gambling, women, and other attractions, but since this was not the case he simply checked into a small hotel on

Sutter Street, which was near enough to the Black Pearl Saloon—and the Barbary Coast—to make it easily accessible.

Of course, the Sutter Street Hotel was small only by San Francisco standards. Anywhere else in the West it would have been considered first rate.

Clint made use of its bath facilities, and when he had freshened up he decided to pay a call on his friends, John Chang and Sam Wing.

The detectives had an office on the outskirts of Chinatown and when Clint arrived there he found it locked and unoccupied. Clint decided that he would try them again later, but at present would visit the home of one other friend he had made last time he was in San Francisco.

Amanda Lincoln lived in a house located near San Francisco's famous "Line," the Market and Kearny Streets section that held all of the city's famous and expensive shops. The two Oriental—actually, *half*-Oriental—detectives had helped Clint out of a tight spot some months back, and Amanda Lincoln had also been a big help. She and Clint had also become *very* friendly.

A similar disappointment awaited Clint as he reached Amanda's house and found that she was not there and the house was locked up tight. He could not tell if she was simply out, or no longer lived there, but he hoped it was the former. He found himself looking forward to seeing the lovely, young blonde woman.

Bearing the brunt of his dual disappointment Clint started back toward his hotel and decided to stop off somewhere for lunch. He hoped to be able to hook up with either the detectives or Amanda between then and the meeting the next day. After lunch, he'd try again.

In a Chinatown hotel that was little more than a hovel, Su Chow did not think that she was going to live long enough to make it to the meeting with the man her brother had told her would help her. She wished that Dan Chow had been able to come himself. Perhaps *he* would have made it in time to save her, but as things appeared now, no one could save her. Not her brother, not the Gunsmith—and not Sam Wing.

The Black Pearl Tong was coming for her, and she had run out of places to hide.

Sam Wing regarded his taller partner, John Chang, sadly and wished he could think of some appropriate words with which to ease his friend's suffering, but he knew that there were no such words in either language, English or Chinese.

John Chang and Sam Wing did not know where Su Chow was, but they did know that she would be at the Black Pearl Saloon the next day—if she was still alive.

They also knew that there was very little chance of that, hence the source of John Chang's suffering: He loved Su Chow deeply.

"Come," Sam Wing finally said, "we will go back to the office. We will not find her stumbling around blindly here in Chinatown."

"We have to keep looking, Sam," John Chang said, looking down along the length of Dupont Street. "We have to!"

Sam Wing shook his head sadly and knew that he would not be able to get his friend to abandon the search until it was obviously hopeless. Rather than tell John Chang what was in his heart Sam Wing said, "Very well, we will keep looking."

Sam Wing had the feeling that Su Chow was already dead—or might as well be.

After lunch, Clint Adams did not find Sam Wing and John Chang at their office, nor did he find Amanda Lincoln home. He'd have only one other opportunity to try, just before the scheduled meeting the following day. He decided to while away the rest of the day and have dinner in Portsmouth Square before going back to his hotel for the evening.

THREE

It was only in the morning when Clint awoke and dressed to go out for breakfast that he realized, looking at the telegram, that there was no time set for the mysterious meeting at the Black Pearl Saloon. He couldn't imagine Su Chow sitting in that saloon all day waiting, so he decided that he was going to have to forgo any attempts to find his friends and go right to the Black Pearl after breakfast.

At the same time John Chang was awakened by Sam Wing in their office. They had slept there in the hopes that Su Chow might show up.

"It's time to go," Wing said. "We don't know what time Su Chow will show up at the saloon."

"Yes," Chang said, sitting up and rubbing his eyes with the heels of his hands, "you're right. I shouldn't have fallen asleep."

"Do not berate yourself for that," Wing said. "It was the best thing for you. It kept you from thinking."

"But not from dreaming," Chang said. "Let's go."

Su Chow was almost frozen with fear at the thought of leaving the hotel she was hiding in, but it had to be done. Getting to the Black Pearl Saloon was the only

9

way she was going to get some help. She had to try, even if she herself doubted that she'd ever make it there alive.

The Black Pearl Saloon was along the lines of a place called the Red Bull Saloon, which Clint had visited on his last visit to San Francisco. It was enormous and filled, and the whores, cutting in and out between the cowboys, businessmen, and Stevedores, were not of the finest quality.

The first thing Clint did was look around to see if he could spot a Chinese girl among the crowd. As early in the day as it was, the Barbary Coast was busy as usual.

When he didn't spot *any* Chinese faces, let alone a woman's, he walked to the bar and ordered a beer, hoping that he wouldn't find anything floating in it. He had it in his hand and was turning to face the room when he saw two men enter the saloon and stopped short.

Not only were they Chinese faces, they were Chinese faces that he knew!

The first thing John Chang did when he entered the Black Pearl was scan the room, looking desperately for Su Chow. Sam Wing's vision was not so selective, however, and the face he spotted stopped him in his tracks. He touched his partner's arm and directed his eyes toward the bar.

"Clint Adams?" John Chang said so that only his partner could hear him. "What's he doing here?"

"Perhaps we should find out," Sam Wing said.

Clint waited until both men were looking at him and

then inclined his head toward the back of the room. He sauntered that way, then, hoping to find at least an empty table, since an isolated one would be a virtual impossibility.

By the time Wing and Chang found their way to the back, Clint had a table and they joined him.

"I've been looking for you two since yesterday," he told them.

"What brings you here?" John Chang almost demanded, eliciting a stare from the Gunsmith.

"Easy, John," Sam Wing said. He looked at Clint and said, "It is important to us that we know what brings you here, Clint. Is it mere coincidence?"

"Are you fellas working on something?"

"Most definitely," Wing said.

"I'm here to meet someone."

"Who?" Chang asked.

"To tell you the truth," Clint said, "I don't rightly know."

"What does that mean?" Chang asked in annoyance.

Clint frowned at the man, puzzled by his attitude, and said, "I'm meeting someone I've never seen before by prearranged appointment. All I've got is a name."

"What is it?" Wing asked.

Clint frowned, not wanting to be difficult but tired of being interrogated.

"Maybe I should ask a few questions at this point."

"Damn it—" John Chang started to explode, but Sam Wing put his hand on his friend's arm to stay his tongue.

"We do not mean to interrogate you, but this is

important to us—perhaps a little more important to John.''

Clint paused a moment, then said, ''What do you want to know.''

''Who are you meeting?''

''A girl named Su Chow.''

''Su?'' Chang said. ''How—Why?''

Clint looked to Wing for an explanation.

''We are also here looking for Su Chow.''

Clint frowned, a firm disbeliever in coincidence.

''What have I walked into here?'' he asked.

''And how?'' Wing added. ''An interesting situation.''

Chang was looking away from the table, studying the crowd, looking for Su Chow.

''I assume you fellas know the girl,'' Clint said.

''Yes,'' Sam Wing said, directing a pointed look at the distracted John Chang. ''How do you know her?''

''I don't,'' Clint said, and explained to Wing how he came to be there waiting for her.

Wing frowned and said, ''Let's assume she sent a telegram to her brother—who neither of us know,'' he said, nodding toward his partner, ''and he in turn sent you a telegram asking you to come here in his stead. Why you?''

''I've asked myself that more than once Sam, believe me. It's not as if we were great friends—''

''And yet you came. Why?''

Clint shrugged.

''I wasn't doing anything in particular . . . and I was curious.''

Sam Wing seemed to accept that.

''Now, how about telling me what I've walked into, and if I'm in the way?''

"I doubt that you could be in the way, my friend," Sam Wing said, "but I will explain."

His explanation was brief. John Chang had met Su Chow while on a case in Chinatown, and the two had fallen in love. What Chang didn't know was that Su Chow was heavily involved with a man who was a member of the Black Pearl Tong. When he did find out, she refused to mention the man's name, but professed once again her love for Chang. Chang asked her to go away with him, and she agreed. She had gone to collect some belongings and had not been seen since.

"That was two weeks ago."

"The girl has been missing since then?"

"Yes."

"Seems to me it would help to know that man's name, the one she was involved with."

"Indeed, yet we have been unable to unearth that piece of information."

"It doesn't seem possible that she could stay holed up that long in Chinatown without someone spotting her."

"Believe me, my friend, we have had all our ears to the ground and have not been able to find her."

"Why hasn't she come to you, Sam. You *and* John."

"I have a theory that she feels she is protecting John by staying away from him."

Clint looked at John Chang, who seemed to have divorced himself completely from the conversation and was busily examining faces.

"So she tried to get help from her brother."

"And he from you. I cannot help but wonder why he could not come himself."

"I can't answer that. Tell me what brought you here today?"

"We finally heard from Su, through a messenger. I think perhaps she has finally decided that she needs our help."

"What can I do to help?"

"Well, we do not know when she intends to come here—if indeed she will be able to. I wish we had known when we entered that you would be offering your help. That help will be somewhat limited, I'm afraid, by the fact that you have been seen here with us under somewhat friendly circumstances."

"Well, we can change that," Clint said.

"How?"

Clint smiled and threw the remains of his beer into the detective's face. John Chang, who had been paying absolutely no attention to the conversation, reacted instinctively to the attack on his partner. He swung his right hand in a chopping motion toward Clint, who was ready for it. He moved so that he took the blow on the chest and then propelled himself backward, knocking over his chair.

Chang stood up to pursue him but again Wing placed a calming hand on his friend's arm—this time with some iron in the grip.

"Enough," he said.

As loud as the place was, the altercation had gone almost unnoticed, save for some tables immediately surrounding theirs. They played to the small audience, however.

"I do not know if I can hold my friend back for very long, stranger," Wing said to Clint as he picked himself up off the floor. Clint thought that the "stranger" might have been laying it on a bit thick, but played along. "I would suggest," Sam Wing continued, "that you leave now."

"Let the slant eyes have it," someone shouted from the crowded room, but Clint ignored the voice. He wiped his hands off on the seat of his pants, stared at the two Chinamen, and then headed for the door, hoping that he looked properly chastised.

"What the hell—" John Chang began.

"Later," Sam Wing said, "later, John."

FOUR

Clint's intention was to meet Wing and Chang at their office later in the evening to find out if Su Chow ever showed up at the saloon. He decided to check Amanda Lincoln's house again to see if she were home. If she were, it would go a long way toward making the time until the evening go by a little more pleasantly.

As he approached the house he immediately noticed a difference. He could *feel* that someone was in the house. He knocked on the door and when it was opened, Amanda Lincoln stood there, looking just as lovely as he remembered.

"Clint Adams," she cried in pure delight, "you son of a bitch!"

"Now what kind of greeting is that?" he demanded, smiling broadly.

"Well, come inside," she said, grabbing him and pulling him into the house. "It gets better."

Amanda Lincoln's husband had been killed by tong members—the Yellow Serpent Society, to be exact—and for that reason she had helped Clint, Sam Wing, and John Chang shut that tong down. He had helped the detectives on several occasions before, and since.

She had long, blond hair, full, firm breasts, and an amazingly *pretty* face.

"Now," she said, approaching him and winging her arms around his neck. She pulled his head down so that she could melt her lips against his, and her tongue was alive inside his mouth. They were both breathless when they broke the kiss.

"If it gets any better than this," Clint said, "it's going to be one hell of a long greeting."

Taking him by the hand she said, "The longer the better," and led him to the bedroom.

He undressed her slowly like a child unwrapping a much awaited present. He peeled her blouse away to expose her magnificent breasts, bending to gently tug each of the nipples with his teeth. His tongue slithered along the valley between her exquisite mounds of flesh, and she sighed and cradled his head in her hands.

He suckled each nipple until they were incredibly hard, and then slid off her skirt and underwear. Without undressing himself he pushed her down to the bed and pressed his lips to the soft flesh of her belly. She continued to cradle and caress his head, urging him lower until his face was buried in the fine patch of hair, his tongue sliding along her moist netherlips.

"Oh, God, yes darling, I've missed you—"

Clint continued to kiss and lick her slipperly slit until he finally concentrated his efforts on the stiffening center of her womanhood. He took it between his lips and alternately sucked and flicked it with his mouth and tongue until he could feel the preparatory tremblings in her belly.

Suddenly she was bucking beneath him. He pinned her thighs to the bed with his elbows while he continued to lick her during her spasms, intensifying them.

"Ohhhh—" she said, drawing it out until she

sounded as if she were growling rather than groaning.

After a few endless moments, when she thought the tremors and waves of pleasure would never stop, she began to murmur, "Please, please, please—" Clint knew she wanted it, and he wanted it just as much.

He raised himself above her and quickly removed his clothes, uncovering his massive, pulsating erection, aching for release. He drove his rock-hard penis into her steaming hot depths; she wrapped her legs around his waist and tightened her grip.

He slid his hands beneath her to cup her smooth, firm buttocks, gripping them whole as he drove into her with long, deep strokes.

"Oh yes, darling, yes," she moaned, "deeper, please, and harder . . . God, yes!"

She began to come again, her moist, hot crater grasping him and virtually yanking his orgasm from him so that they were soaring together.

"I've known John for some time, Clint," she said later as they lay together, her head cradled in the crook of his right arm, "and I'd never seen him this way, so intense. It's a damned shame!" she said, and he could tell by her voice that she was close to tears.

"He was so happy when he found Su Chow, and now that damned tong—"

"Which tong, Amanda?" Clint asked her. "I didn't have a chance to ask Sam. It's not the Yellow Serpent Society again, is it?"

"No," she said, "at least, not under that name. This one appears to be called the Black Pearl Tong."

"Black Pearl?" he asked. "But that's the name of the saloon we were supposed to meet Su Chow at. Why would she choose that place?"

"I don't know, but as far as the boys have been able to discover, there's no connection between the saloon and the tong."

"Don't try and convince me that it's a coincidence," he said in disbelief.

"I know you don't believe in coincidence," she said, "but you'd have to talk to the boys about that."

"I will."

He had already explained to her what had brought him back to San Francisco, and although she had secretly hoped that she had been the reason, she was just glad to have him *back* again—back in her bed and her life, even if she knew that it was not for good.

"Enough talking," she said, rolling over to press her breasts against his chest, flattening them, "and more greetings."

"I don't have to be talked into that," he said, and he couldn't say any more because her mouth was avidly working on his.

FIVE

When Clint left Amanda Lincoln's house he promised that after he spoke to Wing and Chang he'd return to tell her all about it. She was genuinely concerned not only about John Chang, but the girl, Su Chow, as well.

When Clint arrived at the office of Wing and Chang there was a light burning inside. His knock was answered by Sam Wing, who silently invited him in. It took only one look at John Chang's face to tell Clint what he wanted to know.

"She never showed up?"

Wing closed the door and shook his head.

"Is he going to hit me again?" Clint asked, gesturing toward Chang.

"No," Wing said, "I explained to him what happened."

"I'm sorry I didn't explain it to you beforehand," Clint said, "but it was a spur-of-the-moment thing."

"Do not apologize," Sam Wing said, "for thinking quicker than I. Have a seat, I will pour you a drink."

"Thanks."

From the looks of John Chang he had already had quite a few drinks and was staring morosely at about half an inch of liquor that was lying at the bottom of his glass.

"John—" Clint said, just to see if he could get his attention. He did not, and did not try again.

"I don't think he hears us," Sam Wing said, handing Clint a drink, "which is just as well."

"Is this girl that important to him?" Clint asked, watching Chang carefully for a reaction and noting the lack of one.

"Yes," Sam Wing said.

"And what about you?"

"He is my friend—but beyond that, the Black Pearl Tong is in danger of becoming another Yellow Serpent Society. I cannot allow that."

"And when we bring this one down?" Clint asked.

"We?"

Clint nodded and said, "I said it, didn't I."

"When we bring this tong down, another will rise up to take its place, and we will bring that one down, too, and all that come after until there are no others."

"That'll be up to you and John," Clint said. "I won't be here then, but I'm here now, and I'll help you with this one, this Black Pearl Tong. Tell me about it."

"What is there to tell? It has a head and many appendages. We have cut off appendages, but the head remains."

"Then we have to cut off the head."

"First, we must find it."

"How about the saloon?"

"The Black Pearl Saloon?" Wing asked, shaking his head. "A coincidence."

"I don't believe in coincidence," Clint said. "Who owns the saloon?"

"A man named Clark, Howard Clark, but he is *lo-fan*, white. He would not be the head of a tong."

"Why not? Who would suspect it?"

"And if he were, he would not name the tong after his own saloon."

"I repeat, why not? Who would suspect?"

Wing looked annoyed and said, "It is too simple. It could not be so."

"Have you looked into it?"

"We have checked out his past. He appears to be nothing more than a saloon owner. He has owned others in other towns."

"Why did he come here?"

Wing shrugged. "Who stays in one place forever?"

"Not many people, I'll grant you that, but there must be a reason he decided to open a saloon on the Barbary Coast."

"He did not open it. He bought it."

"From who?"

"A dead man's widow."

"Is she still around?"

"No."

"How was the man killed?"

Wing shrugged and said, "How are men killed on the Barbary Coast?"

"Then it wasn't a tong killing?"

"Not by appearances."

"And the Black Pearl Tong appeared after Clark bought and renamed the saloon?"

"Not immediately after, but soon."

"And he did rename the saloon?"

"Yes."

"Well, maybe I should make the acquaintance of Mr. Howard Clark," Clint said. "Why don't you fellas stay away from there for a while and let me see what I can find out?"

"Very well," Wing said. "We will continue to search for Su Chow."

"Why stick to Chinatown?" Clint asked.

"It is where she would hide."

"Expand your search anyway, Sam. It couldn't hurt."

"As you say," Sam Wing agreed, "it couldn't hurt."

Clint finished his drink and waved away the offer of another.

"Is there anyone else I should know about?"

"Yes, someone Su Chow has often mentioned, a woman named Pearl Toy."

"Pearl?"

"Yes," Wing said, frowning. "More and more of those coincidences you so disbelieve in."

"As long as they don't call her 'Black Pearl'," Clint said.

"Not to my knowledge."

"What is it about this woman that makes her of interest to us?"

"Su Chow often said that Pearl had great influence in the Black Pearl Tong."

"A woman with influence in a tong?" Clint asked in disbelief.

"This is what Su Chow said. We do not know how much truth there is to the remark."

"Where would I find Pearl?"

"In Chinatown, in Ross Alley," Wing said. "She runs a very successful whorehouse."

"Owned by the tong?"

"It is very likely."

"Sam, excuse me so for saying so, but you seem to know very little about this tong."

"They have kept a low profile, Clint," the Chinese detective replied in self-defense. "And they have kept their holdings very secretive. We only know about

'Madame Pearl's' because of Su Chow, but she would not tell us very much beyond that about the tong. She was very frightened of its power.''

"What about Kovac?" Clint asked, referring to Chief Inspector Kovac. "Is he still around?" Last time Clint was in San Francisco Kovac had tried to arrest him for the murder of a young Chinese girl, until Clint and the two Oriental detectives were able to prove his innocence.*

"The good inspector is still very much in evidence," Sam Wing said.

"Well, I don't think he'll be too glad to hear that I'm back," Clint said. "I think I'll try to stay out of his way as long as I can."

"A wise course of action."

Clint stood up and said, "Well, I guess I'd better be heading back to my hotel and get a good night's sleep. Tomorrow I'll pay a visit to Mr. Clark at the Black Pearl Saloon and apologize for creating a disturbance in his place of business tonight."

"We will have to continue to meet here, late at night," Sam Wing said, "so that no one will see us together."

"Right. I'll be by tomorrow night after midnight, just to be on the safe side."

Clint threw a look at John Chang and asked Wing, "Is he going to be all right?"

Wing frowned at his friend and said, "I have known John a long time, Clint, and it saddens me to say that I do not really know the answer to that question. I can only hope so."

* The Gunsmith #27: Chinatown Hell

SIX

Instead of going back to his hotel—the thought of which was depressing—Clint decided to keep his promise to Amanda.

"Back so soon?" she asked as she opened the door.

"For some reason I just couldn't stay away," he said, gathering her into his arms and kissing her soundly.

"And what reason was that?" she asked, breathlessly.

"I made you a promise."

"Oh?" she asked. "I had a feeling it was something more . . . *personal* than that."

He looked at her in the floor-length nightgown she was wearing and said, "Why don't we get the promise out of the way first?"

"Good idea," she said, backing away from him, "but first we'll have to put a little space between ourselves or all promises will be forgotten."

"What do you suggest?"

"I know. I'll get you a drink and that'll give you something to hold onto—that is, something *else* to hold onto."

"For a while, anyway."

She smiled and went to get him a glass of whiskey. She handed it to him and when they were seated across from each other asked, "How's John?"

"Terrible," he said. "I've agreed to help Sam find Su Chow and do whatever we have to do to put an end to the Black Pearl Tong—but I'm sorry to say I don't think John Chang is going to be much help. Not unless he comes to his senses."

"I'm sorry to hear that," Amanda said. "John's a good man. I don't know whether to feel sorry for Su Chow for whatever predicament she's gotten herself into, or angry at her for what she's doing to John."

"She's not doing anything to John," Clint said. "John's doing it to himself."

"What do you mean?"

"It's up to a man himself how he's going to react to a crisis, Amanda. How did Harry react to a crisis?" Harry was her dead husband.

"He met it head on."

"That's what John should be doing, meeting it head on instead of crumbling beneath it. I haven't known him as long as you have, but I would have thought he'd handle this thing better than he is."

"So would I," she agreed. "Maybe someone should tell him."

"I assume Sam Wing has. He's his best friend."

"Maybe someone else should tell him."

"I don't know if I'd want to take a chance of getting him mad at me, not with that *wu-shu* stuff he knows."

"I don't think he'd hit me," Amanda said. "Maybe I should have a talk with him tomorrow."

"I wish you would. If we could get him to snap out of it, he'd be a lot more useful."

"I'll do it then," she said, nodding her head once, making up her mind. "What are you going to do?"

"I'm going to poke around a bit and look into a coincidence or two I don't like."

"Like the Black Pearl Saloon?"

"That," he said and went on to explain about Madame Pearl Toy.

"What a hardship for you," she said when he was done, "having to check out a whorehouse. How will you ever stand it?"

"Filthy job that it is, but someone has to do it."

"What an attitude," she said. She got up off the chair she was sitting on and moved toward where he was sitting.

"What are you doing, woman?" he demanded when she dropped herself into his lap.

"Well, if you're going to have to do some extensive investigating in a whorehouse," she said, taking his drink from him and setting it aside, "I figure you're going to need a little practice on your technique."

"Is that a fact?"

"Yes," she said, putting the tip of her nose against his, "it is."

"Well," he said, standing up with her in his arms, "we'll just have to see about that."

She was nibbling on his neck and ear as he carried her into the bedroom.

Clint laid her on the bed and slowly peeled the nightgown over her head. She was naked underneath, and her nipples had already swelled.

He undressed and lay down next to her, directing his attention to her erect nipples. He nibbled on them, sucked them and lashed them with his tongue until Amanda was moaning aloud beneath him, already close to climax. Continuing the oral stimulation of her nipples he reached down between her legs with his right hand and found her wet and waiting. Using his fingers he found her swollen button, and as soon as he touched it, her body was wracked by the spasms of orgasm.

Without waiting for her spasms to cease, he moved his mouth down her body until he was exploring the sweet depths of her with his tongue, prolonging that first orgasm, or possibly launching her directly into a series of sweet explosions until she was begging him, pleading with him to enter her.

"Please, Clint, please, I need it—now!"

His cock was rock-hard and pulsing as he poked at her moist portal with its swollen head, teasing her. She cursed him, reached down and took hold of him and guided him into her. Once he was inside she clasped her arms and legs around him and held tight while he pounded into her violently, seeking his own relief.

"Oh God, darling, yes, harder, as hard as you want—you can't hurt me—"

He took her at her word and continued to pound into her harder and harder until suddenly he reached his own violent climax and filled her with ecstasy.

"So," Clint asked after they had both calmed down, "how was my technique?"

"Mmm," she said, rubbing her palm over his chest in slow circles, "I think I'd have to see it again before I make my final decision."

"Now?" he asked, taking her hand.

"Now," she said, turning toward him, "and later . . . and later and —"

"That could take all night."

She laughed softly, happily, and said, "That's what I had in mind."

SEVEN

In the morning Clint left Amanda still asleep. They had already agreed that he would once again return to her house after talking with Sam Wing and John Chang at midnight. Hopefully, when he did talk with Wing and Chang, he would notice a change in John Chang, as a result of his talk with Amanda Lincoln. Maybe a woman's touch would bring the detective out of it.

He went back to his hotel to take a bath and then over breakfast decided how and when he would approach Mr. Howard Clark. According to Sam Wing, Clark lived in an apartment directly above the saloon, so Clint would have to wait until the afternoon to see him, when the saloon was open.

When Clint returned to his hotel after breakfast he found waiting for him the very man he'd been looking forward to *avoiding*—Chief Inspector Kovac.

The policeman hadn't changed very much. If Clint didn't know any better he'd swear that Kovac was wearing the same tweed suit and derby he'd been wearing the last time Clint had seen him. He had the same dark blond hair, mustache, and mutton-chop sideburns that covered most of his face, and his eyes were just as baggy and tired as ever.

He was also wearing a distinctly unhappy look on his face as Clint stepped into the lobby.

Kovac stepped forward and said, "I was hoping that the report I had gotten was wrong."

"Report about what, Inspector?"

"About your being in San Francisco again."

"Some sharp-eyed policeman of yours?"

"You might remember him," Kovac said. "Calley?"

Clint remembered a young police officer he'd embarrassed by handcuffing him with his own cuffs.

"I remember."

"Well, he remembered you, too. When he told me that he saw you here on the Barbary Coast, I was hoping that he was wrong."

"Well," Clint said happily, "he wasn't, was he?"

"No, he wasn't," Kovac said unhappily. "Adams, what brings you back to my city?"

Clint stifled a trite remark about not having heard about the purchase and said instead, "Can I buy you a drink, Inspector?"

"Only if you'll answer my question while we drink it."

"Of course," Clint said. "Have I ever not cooperated with the police?"

Kovac made a face and said, "Let's go and get that drink. I think I need it."

When they were seated at a table in a nearby saloon—*not* the Black Pearl—Kovac asked his question once again.

"Why are you here?"

"Visiting friends?"

"Those two?"

"What two?"

"You know who I mean. Wing and Chang, those two private detectives."

"That's right. They do live here, don't they?"

"Look, Adams," Kovac said, "I happen to know that those two are up to something. Now what I need to know is if you're working with them."

"Inspector," Clint said, "I'm here to gamble, and to visit friends—like Amanda Lincoln. Check with Miss Lincoln if you don't believe me."

"The President himself could vouch for you, and I still wouldn't believe you."

"That's not very flattering, Inspector."

"If you're here to gamble, what the hell are you doing staying in that dump and not Portsmouth Square?"

"My cash is a little low," Clint explained. "That's why I'm here to gamble. I feel lucky."

"Your story gets worse and worse, Adams," Kovac complained. "You could have found yourself a profitable little poker game anywhere."

Clint started to speak, but Kovac cut him off.

"Never mind," the policeman said. He finished his drink and put the empty glass down on the table. "I can see I'm not going to get a straight answer out of you, so know this: I'm going to have a man watching you the entire time you're here. If you make one false move—"

"How can I do that," Clint asked, "if you're going to have a man watching every move I make? And you know, that could get embarrassing for someone."

"Not for me," Kovac said, standing up, "and that's all I'm worried about." He pointed his index finger at Clint and said, "I've got enough problems without you

showing up now. I won't tolerate any disruptive be-
havior.''

"I'll make a note," Clint said, and Kovac shook his
head in helpless disgust and stormed out of the saloon.

EIGHT

Clint spotted Kovac's man right away, and it took him about that long to lose him. It wasn't necessary to know the town you were in well to lose a tail; all you had to do was pick a crowded street—and there were plenty of those in San Francisco. It also helped that the policeman following him was *not* Calley, who would have had some added incentive to stick with him.

After he lost Kovac's man he decided to go directly to the Black Pearl Saloon to meet Howard Clark. He couldn't be sure he'd ever be that free again.

To his surprise the saloon was open, even though it wasn't eleven yet. Then again, why should he have been surprised? This was the Barbary Coast, after all.

When he entered he found the place about a quarter full mostly with stevedores. He approached the bar and ordered a beer.

"Is the boss around?" he asked when he had his beer.

"Sorry?"

"The boss."

"Mr. Clark?"

"Is he the boss?"

"He owns the place."

"Then he's the man I want to see."

"Listen," the man said, "you ain't a bartender, are

you? We don't need no more bartenders.''

"Your job is safe, Ace," Clint assured the man.
"I'm not a bartender, but I'd still like to see the boss.''

"I'll let him know. Just wait here.''

"Sure.''

Clint nursed his beer while the bartender sent word
to Clark that someone wanted to see him. A few moments later a tall, fair-haired man in his forties came
down the stairs from the second floor and approached
Clint.

"I understand you want to see me about a job?''

"Are you Mr. Clark?''

"That's right.''

"You own the Black Pearl Saloon?''

"That's right," Clark said again, frowning.

"Interesting name—for a saloon, I mean.''

"That was the point," Clark said, "to make the
place sound interesting.''

"What was it called before you changed it?''

"Duff's.''

"Not so interesting.''

"Is this what you wanted to see me about?'' Clark
asked.

"No, not exactly," Clint said. "I didn't tell the
bartender that I was interested in a job . . . but I am.''

"What kind of job?''

"Well, nothing that would find me working in
here.''

"Not in the saloon? What kind of job are you interested in, then?''

"Something with a little more . . . action.''

"I don't understand.''

"Well," Clint said, lowering his voice to a conspiratorial whisper, "I heard that you might be looking for men who were good."

"Good how?"

"You know," Clint said, "with a gun."

"Why would I need someone who was good with a gun?" Clark asked. "I've got bouncers, Mister. What's your name, anyway?"

"Archer."

"Mr. Archer. Why would you think I'd need a man who was good with a gun?"

Clint shrugged and said, "I hit town and I was looking for a job, and I heard you might be interested."

"Well, you heard wrong," Clark said, losing interest. "I've got work to do, if you'll excuse me."

"Oh, sure."

As Clark turned to walk away Clint said, "Oh, one other thing, Mr. Clark."

"Yes?" Clark asked, trying to be patient.

"I wanted to apologize for the little ruckus I caused last night."

"Ruckus? What . . . oh, yes, someone did mention that to me." Clark turned to face Clint again, with a sudden look of interest. "You and two Chinamen had a run-in, right?"

"Yeah," Clint said.

"What was that about?"

"They're a couple of detectives, and I think one of them recognized me."

"Recognized you?" Clark asked. He frowned, and then a look of understanding crept onto his face. "Archer's not really your name, is it?"

"I said it was."

"Sure. Listen, what hotel are you staying in?"

Clint gave him the name of a hotel a couple of blocks from his own.

"I might have something for you after all. Why don't you let me get in touch with you in a day or two?"

Clint eyed Clark for a few moments, then said, "If I wait, will it be worth my while?"

"I think so."

Clint nodded and said, "All right, then. A few days."

"Have another beer on the house," Clark invited. "You'll be hearing from me."

"Thanks."

Clint had another beer on the house, then left to register in that other hotel under the name "Archer."

NINE

After he registered as Archer he went back to his hotel and checked out. He felt it would be better not to be registered anywhere else under his true name. He planned on leaving his things at Wing and Chang's office, but temporarily, he left them at Amanda's.

"You can leave them here longer if you like," she said, eyeing him suggestively.

"I'd like to, but I think it would be safer—and wiser—to leave it at Sam and John's office."

"Are you worried about my welfare," she asked, "or yours?"

"Both."

Actually, as much as he liked Amanda, he didn't want her getting any ideas about his staying round, and to leave his things there could be the start of that.

After leaving Amanda's he went to Chinatown, to Ross Alley, to find Madame Pearl's. Once he got to Ross Alley, he had only to ask someone to receive directions, and he chose a young sailor. Naturally, the man knew exactly where Madame Pearl's whorehouse was.

"Only she calls it a 'Palace of Delight'," the man said. "If I didn't have to get back to my ship I'd take you there, myself."

"Much obliged."

"Ask for Little Chrissie," the man called after him. "She's got a specialty you wouldn't believe."

Clint waved his thanks and kept walking.

When Clint found Madame Pearl's "Palace of Delight" he was surprised at its plain appearance. It looked just like any of the other doors along Ross Alley: thick oak, with the small peephole in the door. It could have been just another gambling room or opium den.

He knocked and the little peep door opened to reveal a pair of eyes of indistinguishable age or sex.

"Madame Pearl's?" Clint asked.

The eyes examined him and apparently found nothing in his appearance to object to. The smaller door closed, the lock slid back, and the large oak door opened.

The opulence on the inside made up for the drab appearance of the outside. The "waiting room" was a large, high-ceilinged room with overstuffed couches and armchairs, on which quite a few gaudily dressed and made up young women sat—some of whom were also overstuffed.

The women wore expensive gowns, many of them sequined, all of them low cut to reveal an overabundance of smooth, firm, perfumed flesh. There didn't seem to be a skinny woman in the lot, and many of them were downright plump.

"Don't worry, Mister," someone said from behind him, "we've got ladies to fit everyone's taste."

He turned and found himself facing a beautiful Oriental woman who seemed to be about eight or ten years older than the rest of the women in the room— most of whom were in their early to mid-twenties.

Clint Adams was a good judge of age, but someone else might have thought her to be as young as the others. Was she one of the "girls" or was she. . . .

"I am Madame Pearl," the woman said, answering his unspoken question. "Welcome to my 'Palace of Delight'." Her English was unaccented and perfect.

"From what I can see it certainly lives up to its name," Clint commented.

"Well, pick one out that you like, and she'll take you upstairs and prove it to you beyond the shadow of any doubt."

Clint Adams had worked himself into a corner, and he knew it. He had never paid for a woman's favors in his life, and he didn't intend to start now, but what was he supposed to tell this woman about why he was there? To "talk" to the girls?

"Well, I tell you," he said, "don't you have any samples around? You know, so I'll have some idea of whether or not my money will be well spent."

"Beforehand?"

"Well, of course. Before I spend my money I want to have some indication that it won't be wasted."

She regarded him silently for a few moments, staring at him curiously. He took the opportunity to examine her a little closer, as well. He would have sworn that she was in her mid-thirties, although she could have easily passed for younger. Her hair was midnight black and, although piled atop her head, he could see that it was very long. Her neck was rather long but elegant, her face heart-shaped. Her body was trim, full at the hips but not in the bust. Still, she was an incredibly desirable, sensuous woman.

"No one has ever come in here asking for a free sample before," she said, breaking into his thoughts.

"There's always a first time."

Looking amused she said, "That makes sense, I suppose."

"I suppose."

Clint recalled his first meeting with a woman called Jade . . .*

"Come to my office," Madame Pearl said finally.

"Madame—" a young Chinese man said, coming up from behind them.

"Later, Lee," she said, cutting him off. "Come with me," she said again to Clint and led the way across the room.

Clint received as many appreciative looks as he handed out as they walked through the room, and he noticed that most of the women were Caucasian. Perhaps most of the Orientals were already engaged in rooms upstairs.

Madame Pearl led him to a door on the other side of the room, opened it, and walked through. As he followed, he thought he heard some of the girls giggling, but couldn't be sure as he closed the door behind him.

The office was small, dominated by a large desk which Madame Pearl circled and sat behind.

"I must take this question of a free sample under consideration," she told him. "Please be seated."

"It's kind of you to take this time with what might be a non-paying customer."

"Not at all. What you say has some merit. On one hand, I would not like to set a precedent by giving you a free sample. On the other hand, if you like what you get you will come back, and you might send others, as well. It would be good for business."

* The Gunsmith #27: Chinatown Hell

Clint looked at her for a few seconds and then said, "I have the impression that you're having fun with me, Madame Pearl."

"Not at all," she said, but the look on her face was still one of amusement. "In fact," she added, standing up, "I will prove it to you."

For a moment Clint thought that the woman was going to approach him and give him the sample herself—but she walked past him to the door, then stopped short of opening it.

"Have you heard anything at all about us?" she asked him.

"Some."

"Would you prefer any particular girl to give you your free sample?"

Clint remembered what the sailor had told him and he said, "How about Little Chrissie?"

"Excellent choice."

"Little Chrissie" turned out to be anything but little. A tall, pretty, buxom blonde with long legs and a large behind, she was what could only be described as a "solidly" built woman.

"This is Little Chrissie?"

"That's what they call me," the woman said, licking her full lips.

Madame Pearl went back behind her desk and said, "We are going to give Mr.—I haven't asked you your name?"

"Archer," he said, giving her the same name he'd given Howard Clark.

"Mr. Archer. We're going to give Mr. Archer a free sample of what we can do."

"Really?" the blonde woman asked, eyeing Clint with interest. "That's almost unheard of."

"Almost?" Madame Pearl said. "It's never been done before, and I expect this to be just between us, Chrissie."

"Of course, Madame," the woman replied, and Clint had the feeling that the big blonde would never even think of mentioning it.

"All right then," Madame Pearl said, "you may proceed, Chrissie."

The blonde approached Clint's chair and he said, "Wait a minute. She's going to do this with you in the room?"

"But of course. We are setting a dangerous precedent here, Mr. Archer. I intend to be here to see it. Go ahead, Chrissie."

The blonde went down to her knees and ran her hands along Clint's thighs, moving toward his crotch.

"Hang on a second—" Clint started to object, but Madame Pearl overrode his objection.

"These are the only conditions under which you will get your free sample, Mr. Archer. Take it or leave it," she said, the amused look once again on her face.

Clint thought that she expected him to leave it, so he smiled and said, "I'll take it."

She hid her surprise well, blinking once before telling Chrissie, "Proceed."

Chrissie seemed amused by the whole thing as she ran her hands along Clint's thighs and eventually pressed one hand against the bulge in his pants. Clint, who had originally thought having Madame Pearl sitting there watching would inhibit him, actually had a raging erection at the thought.

Chrissie, cooing and licking her lips, seemingly unaffected by the presence of her boss, opened Clint's pants, reached in and drew out his erection, which was engorged and pulsing. She murmured appreciatively and pressed it to her cheek, reaching in again and this time freeing his swollen balls. Clint had moved his hips in order to assist her, and now she was fondling his balls with one hand while rolling his shaft from cheek to cheek, occasionally making a flicking motion with her tongue, barely touching him, yet sending shock-waves of pleasure through him with each flick.

While Chrissie played with his swollen member Clint stared at Madame Pearl, who was watching him with a bemused, interested look on her face. He knew that all she could see from her vantage point was the back of Chrissie's head, and he wondered if she weren't just the least bit curious about what the blonde woman had to play with.

Suddenly, Clint felt the hot ring of Chrissie's mouth fall over him, taking first the head into her mouth, and then much of the shaft. Her tongue began to play along the underside, then swirled around the top. Slowly her head began to bob up and down, her mouth riding him, and he reached to cup her head in his hands without breaking eye contact with Madame Pearl.

Chrissie was using one hand to tickle the inside of his thighs, the other to encircle the base of his cock while she continued to work on him with everything at her disposal—her mouth, her tongue, her teeth, and the movement of her head.

She teased him to incredible fullness—aided by the presence of Madame Pearl—and then began to suck him, squeezing his balls lightly. Clint imagined what her head must look like bobbing up and down in his lap, and then he began to fantasize that it was Madame Pearl's head, and not Chrissie's, and that seemed to bring him dangerously close to completion. Chrissie expertly sensed that he was about to explode and tightened the ring of her fingers around the base of his cock, repressing his approaching orgasm, which caused him both intense pleasure and indescribable pain.

His penis felt as if it had swelled to incredible proportions, and still she would not allow him to come. The strain probably began to show on his face because Madame Pearl was looking more and more amused at his dilemma. She knew that he didn't want to be the one to break their eye contact, yet Chrissie wasn't making that easy for him. Then again, Clint noticed something about her, too. There were beads of perspiration on her upper lip, and her breathing had increased. Despite her calm, inscrutable appearance, she was sexually aroused.

Chrissie was making sounds now, moaning and loud sucking noises, and suddenly the tightening ring of her fingers disappeared. Clint literally exploded. He didn't move his eyes away from Madame Pearl's, but quite involuntarily he had to close them against the waves of pleasure that were wracking his body. His hands were tangled in Chrissie's hair and when he realized it, he released her for fear he'd been hurting her.

"Don't worry, honey," Chrissie said, patting her hair back into place and licking her lips with a satisfied look, "you didn't hurt me at all."

"That will be all, Chrissie," Madame Pearl said coldly.

Was there a hint of jealousy in her tone? Or envy?

"Thank *you*," Chrissie said to her boss *and* to Clint and left the room.

Clint's legs were still weak as Madame Pearl smiled at him and asked, "So, what do you think?"

"Jesus," he gasped, remembering what the sailor

had told him, "I wonder what her specialty is."

Madame Pearl laughed musically and said, "My dear, that *was* her specialty."

Madame Pearl poured Clint some of her fine brandy.

"You seem to have the very best of everything here."

"Oh, yes," Madame Pearl said, "that's part of our . . . appeal."

"A small part, I'm sure," Clint said. "I've just experienced the largest part."

"Chrissie," Madame Pearl said. "Yes, she is probably the best girl in the house, but the others are almost as good."

"I'm sure," Clint said, "but I'm not all that sure that Chrissie is the best in the house."

Madame Pearl smiled and said, "Flattery."

Clint put his empty glass down on her desk and said, "No, just a feeling I have."

"Really?" Madame Pearl asked, unable to hide the pleased look on her face.

"Yes, and if I had the time—or the energy—we could find out if I'm right."

He started for the door and she said, "Oh, I'm sure you have the energy, Mr. Archer."

"Maybe," he said, "but not the time." He opened the door and added, "but I'll come back when I do."

"Is that a promise?"

"You can count on it."

TEN

When Clint spotted the man following him from Madame Pearl's, he assumed it was one of Kovac's men and made no attempt to lose the man.

Leaving Madame Pearl's self-proclaimed "Palace of Delight" Clint was a bit unsure as to where to go from there. He was not sure he could really be that much help. San Francisco was not his town, and he really didn't know what he could do beyond what he'd already done until he spoke to the two detectives again. He'd established himself to some degree with Howard Clark and with Madame Pearl, now all that remained was to sit back and see what, if anything, developed from his new acquaintances.

Thinking of new acquaintances made Clint check to see if the man was still following him. It was early evening in Chinatown, not yet dark, and the streets were still busy. He probably could have lost the man if he wanted to, but since he wasn't going anyplace in particular, it wasn't worth the effort. Later, when he went to see Wing and Chang at their office, he'd make the effort to lose him.

As it turned out, he should have lost the man right away.

Why they waited until he'd left Chinatown and

49

reached the Barbary Coast he didn't know, unless they were just more at home there.

The hotel he'd registered in as Archer was a rattrap, to say the least, but he wanted to go back at least to check for a message from Clark. The man following him positioned himself across the street as Clint entered and inquired of the clerk whether or not there were any messages.

"Whatta I look like," the clerk demanded, "a post office?"

The man was small and wiry and had a prominent Adam's apple. Clint's first instinct was to squeeze it, but he he held himself in check.

"Just look in my box, friend, and tell me what you see—while you can still see."

The man glared at Clint for a moment, then reluctantly turned and directed his glare into Archer's box.

"I don't see nothing," he said, not without a certain degree of satisfaction.

"Thanks. My compliments on your hotel's excellent service."

When he left the hotel the man he thought was a policeman was standing across the street, arms folded across his chest. He was not a tall man, but was very wide across the chest and shoulders. Clint turned and started down the street without bothering to check and see if the man was following him. He knew he was.

Clint chose a small side street to use as a shortcut to Amanda's house, and that's when he realized he'd made a mistake regarding the man who was dogging his trail. Apparently, there had been another man in front of him all the time as well. The two men knew what they were doing, because he never guessed about the second man until it was too late.

He was halfway down the street when someone

suddenly stepped out of a doorway from his right. The blow was too swift for him to react to properly, but his natural reflexes enabled him to avoid its full force. As it was, it struck him on the point of the right shoulder, effectively paralyzing his right arm and hand.

He didn't know exactly what he'd been hit with, but he knew that it hurt like hell, and that he wouldn't be able to use his right arm to defend himself—or draw his gun. He threw himself into the street in the hopes of avoiding further punishment and took a look behind him to see how the "policeman" was reacting to his dilemma. The man was rushing toward him, but from the look on his face Clint knew it wasn't to help him.

He staggered to his feet and started running down the street. Both men were out to cause him grievous bodily harm, and that knowledge added wings to his feet.

As he ran he reached across his body with his left hand to draw his gun from its holster. Although he was fairly proficient with his gun left-handed, he was not ambidextrous and hated to depend on his left hand to save his life. Instead of turning and facing the two men who were obvious professionals, he decided to keep running and use the gun as a last resort.

As he turned the corner from the street he heard a shot and a chunk of hot lead whizzed past his ear. He wondered why they had not fired at him sooner, rather than just trying to disable him. Were they simply out to rob him?

Both men fired at him at the same time. They had also rounded the corner and were right behind him. Reaching behind with his left hand and pulling the trigger twice Clint fired blindly. The two men dropped back quickly.

While he ran, his right arm began to tingle as life

started returning to it. If he could stay ahead of them long enough, he'd eventually be able to turn and face them with his gun in his right hand.

As he ran through the Barbary Coast—virtually ignored, since running and shooting were not out of the ordinary there—he suddenly realized that they had not fired at him for at least two blocks. By this time he was able to clench and unclench his right hand weakly, and he transferred the gun to that hand.

Digging in with his heels he stopped and turned quickly, gun held loosely in his hand.

A few people were staring at him, but for the most part no one seemed particularly interested in him, and there was no one pointing a gun at him.

They had obviously given up the chase, but where had they gone?

Clint was standing in the middle of the street, a perfect target if the men were taking a bead on him from hiding at that moment, so he holstered his gun and stepped up on the boardwalk. He continued to walk toward Amanda's house, being very careful to travel busy streets rather than shortcuts through deserted ones. He continued to work his right hand and arm in an effort to throw off the effects of the earlier blow, and by the time he reached his destination there was only a dull ache in his shoulder to remind him of it.

Amanda immediately divested him of his shirt so she could examine his shoulder and found a bruise right over the bone.

"I shouldn't have come here," he said again, for the four or five hundredth time.

"Forget it," she said again. "You probably scared them silly firing back at them. Hold still."

She pressed on his shoulder and he said, "Ouch."

"It's just bruised," she assured him.

"Well, keep trying," he said. "You'll break it yet."

"Don't be a baby," she said, running cool hands over his shoulders and chest. She pressed her lips to the back of his neck, reached lower with her hands, and said, "Mmm, baby."

"I've just barely escaped grievous bodily harm," he said, scolding her, "and may have brought my assailants to your door, and all you can think about is . . . hey, don't do that—"

"Why not?"

"It tickles."

"Mmm," she said, biting the side of his neck, "then tickle me."

On the way to the bedroom Clint took a quick look out the window and was satisfied to find no one watching the house. He only had time for a brief look before Amanda pulled him forcibly into her bed.

"So tell me," she said sometime later.

"Tell you what?"

"What you've been up to. Did this attack have anything to do with John Chang's girl friend, Su Chow?"

"I honestly don't know," Clint said, frowning. "When the man started following me from Madame Pearl's—"

"Madame Pearl's?" Amanda asked, lifting her eyebrows.

"Uh, yeah, I, uh—"

"Don't stammer, Clint," she said. "Go on with your story."

"When he picked me up I thought he was a policeman, one of Kovac's men. I guess I was wrong about that, but I still don't know who they *were*."

"Well, then I guess you'll just have to go out and find out, won't you? I mean, that's what men like you do, isn't it?"

"What do you mean?"

"You're not going to sit still for being attacked and chased down the streets of the Barbary Coast, are you?"

"No, of course not."

"That's what I mean, then," she said. "You, Sam Wing, and John Chang are going to go out there and try to save Chinatown, the Barbary Coast, and all of San Francisco.

"So?"

"So, damn it, make love to me one more time before you go," she said, "because I'll be damned if I know when I'll see any of the three of you alive again."

ELEVEN

Clint dallied with Amanda until almost midnight, and then left to go to Sam Wing and John Chang's office. As he left Amanda's house he felt a weakness in his knees, due no doubt to the session with Little Chrissie at Madame Pearl's and the past few hours spent with Amanda. Pleasant hours, to be sure, but also very tiring. She told him to come back after he spoke to the detectives, but he was going to have to think twice about that.

When he reached the detective's office he found that they were not there, and the door was locked, but Sam Wing had slipped him an extra key the last time they met, and he used it to let himself in.

The pleasant weariness was still there as he sat on the office couch and the next thing he knew he was being jostled awake.

"Come on, Clint," John Chang said, looming above him. "This isn't a flophouse, you know."

"John—" Sam Wing said from behind him.

Chang shrugged and moved away from Clint to his desk, where he began to look through the drawers for something.

"Sorry I dozed off," Clint said to Wing, standing up.

"Forget it. You must have had a rough day."

"You don't know the half of it."

At the desk Chang finally found what he wanted, producing a half-filled bottle of bourbon.

"Anyone?" he asked, holding it aloft.

"No, thanks," Clint said, and Sam Wing simply shook his head.

"You fellas don't look like you've had any luck today," Clint said to both men.

Chang lowered the bottle and said, "Now *you* don't know the half of it."

"It was a bit fruitless, to say the least," Wing agreed. "How did your day go?"

"You tell me," Clint said and proceeded to outline his meetings with Howard Clark and Madame Pearl. Of course, he left out the session with Chrissie and what he and Amanda had done was their own business.

"Doesn't sound like a heck of a lot," John Chang said when he was finished.

"Well, that all depends, John," Clint said.

"On what?"

"On what Howard Clark's connection with the tong is."

"If any."

"Forgive John, Clint," Sam Wing said. "He's a little pessimistic these days. Rest assured we appreciate the help you're giving us."

"Well, I don't know how much help I'm being," Clint said. "For one thing, this is not exactly my town, although I know enough to get around. I think the only thing I can do now is sit back and see what the seeds I've planted today will sow."

"At least you've planted," Sam Wing said.

"And they've already brought me one thing."

"What?"

Clint told Sam Wing about the attack on him, and the chase through the streets of the Barbary Coast.

"Do you think they were sent by someone? Howard Clark, perhaps?" Sam Wing asked.

"That remains to be seen, I guess," Clint said. "They could have simply been out to rob me. After all, one of them did follow me from Madame Pearl's, which could be their method of operation."

"But you don't think that, do you?"

"It doesn't feel right," Clint admitted. "Again, I think I'm just going to have to wait at my hotel and see what happens. Either Clark will send for me and offer me a job, or there'll be another attempt on me."

"What about Madame Pearl?" Wing asked. "How does she fit into all this?"

"I'm not sure, but I am sure of one thing," Clint said, "and that is that we'll be seeing one another again."

"She's a dangerous lady, Clint. Be careful."

"Do you know her?"

Wing nodded and added, "And she knows us."

"That means we'll have to keep meeting out of the public eye."

"That's fine with me."

"Me, too," John Chang said, setting his bottle down with a bang. "We'll have to make sure we have more whiskey, though."

"None for me, thanks," Clint said, trading glances with Wing, who shrugged helplessly. This was obviously a situation Sam Wing had never encountered, and he wasn't at all sure how to handle it.

"I should tell you that I've changed hotels and registered under another name," Clint said to Wing.

"Not Murphy, I hope?"

"No," Clint said, remembering what had happened the last time he'd used his friend Murphy's name, "not Murphy. I made one up this time."

"What is it?"

"Archer," Clint said, thinking briefly of two women in his life with that last name. J. T. Archer and Anne Archer were not related, and probably did not know each other, but each of these young women held a special place in Clint's past. He hadn't consciously been thinking of either of them when he chose the name, but he thought of them now.

Clint told Sam Wing the name of the hotel he was in now and said, "I thought it better to keep my real name out of it, at least for now."

"Smart," John Chang said. The level on the bottle had decreased by half since he'd unearthed it. "I always said ole Clint was smart."

Clint wished he could pull Sam Wing aside and talk privately, but given John Chang's present state, he was sure the man wouldn't react well to such an action.

"I'll see you fellas tomorrow night, then," Clint said. "If you need me, try my hotel or leave a message with Amanda. I'll do the same if I need you."

"Right," Wing said. "Amanda will be our post office, but I would not like to get her involved beyond that."

"I agree," Clint said.

"Sure," Chang chimed in, "we've lost one girl already, why risk another?"

It was the only thing he'd said since their arrival that made any sense.

There was hope of his coming out of it, yet.

Clint decided to go back to the hotel rather than go

back to Amanda's house. If Howard Clark was looking for him, he wanted to be easy enough to find, and that meant staying on the Barbary Coast. He only hoped that Kovac and his men wouldn't locate him first.

Of course, the need for a good night's sleep also had something to do with his decision. He certainly wouldn't get that in Amanda's bed.

Not by a damned sight.

TWELVE

The two men who had attacked and chased Clint Adams were in the back office of the Black Pearl Saloon, reporting the results of their efforts. They had been instructed not to come to the back door of the saloon until midnight and were let in by Howard Clark himself.

"Is the man here?" the first man asked. His name was Fitzgerald but everybody called him "Fitz." He was the man who had followed Clint from Madame Pearl's.

"No," Clark replied. "You'll have to make your report to me."

"Can we get a drink?" the second man asked. His name was Garvey, and he was the man who hit Adams with his gun.

"Help yourself," Clark said, indicating the sideboard that held a few liquor bottles, as well as a crystal decanter filled with some fine brandy. He watched with bated breath as both men approached the liquor, then breathed a sigh of relief when they ignored the brandy and each took a glass of whiskey.

"Have a seat," Clark said when they both had their drinks. "Tell me what happened."

It was Fitz who related the incident to Clark, telling him exactly what happened without holding anything back.

"Sounds like he did all right, then," Clark summed up.

"He was lucky," Garvey said in disgust.

"Sounds to me like you were lucky," Clark said. "From what you said I figure he let you chase him until the feeling started to come back in his arm, and then he turned on you and scared you away."

"He didn't scare nobody," Garvey said testily.

Fitz was calmer about it, but he too protested Clark's choice of words.

"You told us to back off as soon as he showed some resistance."

"So I did."

Both men remained silent, expecting Howard Clark to go on, and when he didn't the silence began to get awkward.

"Have you got anything else to add?" Clark finally said, breaking the silence.

"No," Fitz said. Garvey shook his head, looking sullen.

"Finish your drinks, then. That'll be all for now."

"Money," Garvey said.

Clark looked annoyed and said, "Of course."

He opened the top drawer of his desk and drew out two brown envelopes. He reached across his desk and handed one to each man. Fitz held his in his lap, but Garvey counted his and grunted his satisfaction when he found all the hundred was there.

"If you need us again—" Garvey started to say.

"I'll let you know."

Both men put their glasses down on the desk, stood up, and walked to the back door. Clark let them out, and then locked the door behind them.

"He could have said thanks," Garvey complained.

"We got paid, didn't we?" Fitz said. "Be satisfied with that."

"Who does he think he is, anyway?"

"He knows who he is, and so do we," Fitz said, waving his envelope. "He's the man with the money, and that's all we need to know."

Garvey grinned and said, "Yeah. Now let's go and spend some of it."

"I'm for that."

And both men knew that meant one thing—Madame Pearl's.

Howard Clark went back to his desk and frowned at the dirty glasses on his desk. He left them there and went to the sidebar to pour himself a snifter of that fine brandy.

Archer hadn't panicked, which was satisfactory, and after his arm had come back, he had retaliated, which was also satisfactory. From the way Fitzgerald had described the blow struck by Garvey, Clark knew that Archer's arm had to have gone dead, or the man might have killed one or both of them.

Clark was tired of employing Barbary Coast sludge, all of whom thought that he was the tong leader's right-hand man. What Clark needed, however, was a right-hand man of his own, and perhaps this man Archer would fit the bill.

All he had to do was check him out a little further now, before talking to him again. If all went well, the man might be just what Howard Clark was looking for.

If it didn't work out, then the man was simply dead.

THIRTEEN

As it turned out, Clint Adams spent a fitful night with his gunbelt hanging on the bedpost, a boot full of change on the windowsill, and a small end table pushed up against the door, with a pitcher perched right on the edge so that the slightest vibration would send it crashing to the floor.

He was in a café on his second pot of coffee when he realized that he'd left something untended to. When he'd registered in his present hotel he had put his address down as Labyrinth, Texas, a town that had become something of a home base for the Gunsmith. Of course, before Clark made any move to hire him he'd have to check him out, which would mean sending a telegram to Labyrinth. Clint knew that he should have sent a telegram himself to his friend, Rick Hartman, to set up a story for Mr. "Archer."

After breakfast he found the nearest telegraph office, carefully worded a message, and had it sent on to Labyrinth, addressed to Rick Hartman. By now his friend Rick was used to receiving such telegrams and usually knew how to react to them.

That done, Clint found himself in the same position he'd been in the night before, that of being at loose ends as to what to do with himself. He decided to do some gambling, and where else would a man gamble in

San Francisco but Portsmouth Square, where all of the big gambling houses were located.

When Clint entered the Alhambra Saloon his only intention was to gamble. He had not, however, decided where to start—roulette, faro, poker? Poker had always been his pleasure, but tonight he felt like trying something else. He was surveying the room, trying to decide, when he saw the woman.

His initial surprise was simply because she was Oriental, but that passed quickly, overcome by the sheer, exquisite beauty of her.

She was small, as most Oriental woman were, and she had the long, black hair that most Oriental women did. But in some unfathomable way she was different from other Chinese women he'd met—including Madame Pearl, who had her own peculiar brand of appeal.

The woman wasn't gambling, but the man she was in the company of was. They were standing at the faro table, the man engrossed in the game, and the woman standing quietly at his side.

Clint decided to take a moment to look the man over, as well. He was tall, expensively dressed, apparently in his mid-twenties, and in what appeared to be good physical condition. Clint couldn't see a gun, but he was willing to bet that the man had one, possibly in a shoulder or sleeve rig.

Having surveyed his objective, and his competition, Clint descended the steps into the gaming room and approached the faro table.

"You are bringing me remarkably good luck, my dear," he heard the man say as he came alongside the woman.

"I am pleased, Jonathan," the woman said in a remarkably throaty voice. Clint thought that she sounded somewhat less than pleased, and that was music to his ears.

He stood next to her for a few moments, observing the play of her man friend, and waited for her to look at him. When she made no move to focus her eyes on anything—including him—he decided that more direct actions would be necessary.

Faro was a relatively simple card game, and probably the favorite card game of the West. On the table before them was the faro layout, or the "spread," showing reproductions of all thirteen cards in the deck. The cards in this spread were spades, but the suit had no bearing on the bets made. A player backed a card by laying a chip on the reproduction. The dealer dealt one card from his dealing box, which was the loser, and then a second card, which was the winner. Bets made on cards that did not show were either left on the table for the next round or removed. At a player's own discretion, he could either bet a card to win, or to lose. If he bets it to lose, it must be the first card out of the box. If he bets to win, it must be second.

Theoretically speaking, a player could keep count of the cards that had appeared and the cards that were left in the dealing box, and place his bets accordingly. Other players were just plain lucky, and this man Jonathan seemed to be in that class. Clint Adams preferred to use skill in anything he did whether it was gambling, making love, or guns.

Clint waited until the dealer inserted a new deck into the dealing box and then began to keep count. At one point, he began to make bets on which cards would lose, as Jonathan kept guessing which ones would win.

The other man was guessing two out of five, while Clint—with the help of a certain amount of luck, of course—hit four out of his first five bets. He hit three of his next five, and then three again. By this time he had attracted a certain amount of attention around the table—including that of the Oriental woman standing next to him.

While everyone at the table expected Clint to keep playing his incredible "luck", he knew it couldn't last forever—especially if the dealer realized that he was keeping track of the cards and started to cheat.

He quit while he was ahead, and the other gamblers at the table turned their attentions elsewhere, looking for the next hot player. Clint knew, however, that he had successfully attracted the attention of the Oriental woman. Unfortunately, he had also attracted her escort.

"Excuse me, sir," the man said.

"Yes?"

"I couldn't help but notice how well you were doing," Jonathan said. "Why did you stop?"

"A smart gambler always knows when to stop, friend."

"Yes," the other man said, "I suppose so, but I'm afraid I'm not a very smart gambler. Just a lucky one." He put his hand out and said, "My name is Jonathan Biggs, and I would very much like to buy you a drink."

Clint collected the hand into his own without hesitation and said, "Archer, and I accept."

"Excellent. Let's go into the dining room, then. My dear?" he said to the woman, who merely nodded and allowed him to guide her. Clint followed, enjoying the view of the woman from the rear.

It wasn't until they were seated that Biggs introduced his companion, and not without a certain degree of smugness at having such a creature on his arm.

"This lovely young lady is Miss Lisa Lee, Mr. Archer. She is my . . . companion." The pause was deliberate, meant to indicate that she was much more.

"For the evening?" Clint asked hopefully, seeking clarification.

Biggs looked smug again as he said, "For as long as I want, isn't that right, my dear?"

"Whatever you say, Jonathan."

Clint couldn't help but wonder just what their relationship was? Was he paying for her? Or was she simply devoted to him?

Biggs ordered a bottle of champagne, saying that he wished to toast to new friends. Clint thought the man was too smooth a talker, but figured that he had to have something on his mind.

On the surface, the evening passed rather pleasantly. However, there were underlying currents, most of them passing between Clint and Lisa Lee. Jonathan Biggs seemed totally unaware of it, which was a tribute to his monumental ego. It never occurred to him that while she was with him Lisa Lee could become interested in another man.

Clint found out that Biggs was the son of a wealthy rancher who spent most of his time spending his father's hard-earned money. Biggs had no qualms in admitting that about himself.

"My dear father is very good at making money," he said candidly, "while I am equally as good at spending it."

"What is Miss Lee good at?" Clint asked, without thinking.

Biggs didn't seem to mind the question.

"She helps me spend it."

Clint nodded and exchanged glances with her while Biggs was looking for their waiter to order another bottle of champagne.

Clint had the distinct impression that although Jonathan Biggs definitely had first-class money, looks, and manners, he was not anywhere near the class of his escort.

Clint decided to leave and as he started to rise Biggs looked at him and said, "Where are you going? I've ordered another bottle of champagne."

"Not for me, thanks. I've got a little more gambling to do, and then I've got to get back to my hotel. I've got an early day tomorrow."

"Are you staying here?" Lisa Lee asked.

He looked directly at her because it was the first time she had addressed him directly.

"No," he said, and did not elaborate on where he was staying. That would not have impressed her at all. She stared at him boldly for a moment, then slowly averted her eyes.

"Will we be seeing you around here again, later this week, perhaps?" Biggs asked.

"That's possible," Clint said, and the look he gave Lisa Lee said that it was much more likely that he'd be seeing *her* around. Her look said she agreed. Biggs was seemingly oblivious to the entire exchange.

"If we do see you again, Mr. Archer, perhaps I can arrange for you to come and see my father's ranch. We can have a drink there."

"Or a few."

"Yes," Biggs said, laughing, "a few."

"I'd enjoy that. Good night," he said to both of them.

"Good night, Mr. Archer," Biggs said, and Lisa Lee simply inclined her head.

As Clint walked away from the table Biggs said, "That's an interesting man, don't you think?"

Lisa Lee gave Biggs a blank look and said, "I did not notice, Jonathan. Where is that other bottle of champagne?"

FOURTEEN

Clint was seated at the poker table, well ahead of the game, when Lisa Lee appeared again. She directed a pointed look his way and he played out the hand that was in progress, and then excused himself from the game.

"Hope you'll be coming back to give us a chance to get some of that back," a man seated across from him said.

"I'll be back," Clint said, raking in his chips.

He cashed in his winnings and then approached Lisa Lee, who was standing quite still, waiting for him.

"What happened to Jonathan?" he asked.

"He opened one bottle of champagne too many," she said. "I've sent him home."

"I see."

"I've taken a room."

"You don't waste any time."

"Neither do you. I know you wanted me when you first walked in, and you set out to get me. Are you saying now that you don't want me?"

"I'm not saying that at all," Clint said. "I would never say that. Lead the way."

He followed her up to the second floor and into a suite. Once they were in the room she turned to face him and her face was almost as inscrutable as it had been downstairs. Her expression was the same, but she was breathing faster and her face had a flushed look. As he approached her, her nostrils flared, and when he closed his arms around her she seemed to go limp in his arms and simply said, "Yes!"

When he kissed her she seemed to catch fire, clawing at his clothes while sucking wildly on his tongue. The taste and smell of her was heady. He had been with many women in his life and didn't know if this one was different because she was Chinese, or simply because she *was* different from other women. Whatever it was, his hands worked quickly at her clothing, just as her hands were working feverishly on his.

Her breasts, when he'd bared them, were full, round, and warm in his hands. The nipples were dark brown and swollen to incredible size. He pushed her back so that she fell onto the oversized bed and then tumbled to the mattress with her, careful not to let his entire weight crush her.

First his mouth sought her breasts and nipples, sucking and nibbling at them eagerly while she writhed beneath him, murmuring to him in singsong Chinese.

Her skin was incredibly smooth and firm as he kissed and nipped his way down her body, pausing to probe her navel with his tongue and then going further still until his tongue was avidly seeking the taste of her love juices.

His first taste of her made him almost desperate for more, and he began to drive his tongue deeper inside of her while she gripped the back of his head tightly and drove her hips into his face in response to the pressure. Her singsong Chinese mutterings had become higher in pitch and volume until, as he found her love button and worked her toward a shattering orgasm, she began to babble aloud in a mixture of Chinese and English.

When he felt her belly begin to tremble, he used his elbows to pin her thighs to the bed, and she stiffened as the massive orgasm took hold of her. Being unable to move her hips seemed to intensify the sensations, and she started drumming her fists on the mattress and tossing her head from side to side.

When Clint felt her tremblings begin to decrease he released the hold he had on her thighs and moved up so that his erection was prodding the slippery, slick portal between her legs. She opened her thighs anxiously, gasping as Clint drove himself deep into her.

Her frenzied movements had caused her hair to fall across her face like a dark, black curtain, in some places becoming plastered to her skin by her perspiration. Clint used one hand to draw the hair away from her face, and he was slightly taken aback by what he saw. The look on her previously inscrutable face was now one of pure lust. She was biting her lips, her nostrils were flaring, and her eyes were wide open. As much as he was giving her she wanted more, and in an effort to get it she gripped his buttocks and drove her nails into his flesh. He slid his hands beneath her to cup her rounded cheeks and from that point on they could not have gotten closer.

As he continued to take her in long, fast, hard strokes he began to realize that the sounds she was making were no longer words of any language. She was simply moaning and crying out loud, and as he felt her starting to reach her climax he abandoned any semblance of self-control and went over the edge with her.

The period immediately following was somewhat awkward. They were both caught somewhat by surprise at how intense their coupling had been.

Finally, she said, "I must go."

"Fine," he said.

She started to get dressed, then turned as if she were going to say something, but hesitated before saying, "Will we see each other again?"

He stood up and began to dress also.

"Maybe. Can I ask you a question?" he asked.

"If you like. I will answer it if I can."

"What's your relationship with Jonathan Biggs?"

She finished dressing and then stared at him, her face once again devoid of any emotion.

"If we should meet again," she said, walking to the door, "ask me then."

"Will you answer then?"

She gave him a last look before walking out the door and said, "Probably not . . . but you may ask."

When Clint left Portsmouth Square he went back to his hotel to check for messages. When he convinced the clerk to check his box and discovered that there were none, he went to Sam Wing and John Chang's office. Sam Wing was there alone.

"Where's John?"

Wing looked at Clint and shrugged his shoulders helplessly.

"I wish I knew, Clint."

"What happened?"

"We separated at one point today. He said he wanted to be alone for a while, and that was the last I saw of him."

"That's not like him."

"He hasn't been the same man for some time."

"Since Su Chow's disappearance?"

Sam Wing waved away Clint's words impatiently and said, "Since before that. Ever since he first got involved with Su Chow he has not been the same. Now, it has simply become more extreme."

"And now he's gone—maybe dead?"

"I hope not," Wing said. "If he is dead he will not have died easily. There would be some sign."

"Maybe we should talk to Kovac."

Wing laughed almost contemptuously and said, "Inspector Kovac would not talk to me."

"He'll talk to me."

"What makes you think so?"

"I have a feeling he's been looking for me. Maybe it's time I let him find me, again."

FIFTEEN

"You!" Kovac exploded when Clint Adams entered his office. "I've had my men out looking for you ever since you—"

"Lost them?"

"What—"

"Come on, Kovac. I knew you had at least one man following me, maybe more. It's not my fault they couldn't keep up with me."

"It isn't?"

Clint spread his hands in a gesture of honesty.

"You don't think I deliberately lost them, do you?" he asked. "They're trained men."

"Never mind," Kovac said in annoyance. "Now that I've got you I'm going to keep you."

"On what charge?"

"I don't need a charge."

"Come on, Kovac. Why don't you stop trying to scare me and talk to me."

"About what? All I want you to do is stay out of trouble in my town, Adams, that's all. If you want trouble, go someplace else."

"I will—"

"Good!"

"—as soon as I find a couple of friends of mine."

"What friends?"

79

"A girl named Su Chow and John Chang."

"Chang? What the hell happened to Chang?"

"He disappeared."

"I'm heartbroken."

"He might be dead."

"That would be a shame," Kovac said in a tone of voice that clearly said he felt otherwise.

"Kovac, what have you got against those two, anyway?"

"One thorn in my side would be enough," Kovac said, "but they give me one on each side, and then you show up. I'd like to put you all in a cell."

"What would that accomplish?" Clint demanded. "Look, a young Chinese woman is mising, maybe dead; John Chang is missing, maybe dead, and the Black Pearl Tong is involved."

"Oh, Je-sus!" Kovac shouted. He slammed his hands down on his desk and stood up. "I knew it! What the hell are you, Adams, some kind of tong breaker? Everytime you get bored with your life are you gonna come to my town and pile up some bodies for me?"

"I didn't start it, Kovac."

"Well, pardon me all to hell! That makes all the difference in the world."

They stood glaring at each other for a few long moments, and then Kovac sat down.

"Have a seat, Adams."

Clint sat down.

"You want to tell me why you came to San Francisco?"

Clint explained about the telegram he got, about Dan Chow and Su Chow, and how he'd innocently run into Wing and Chang working on the same case.

"You want me to believe that you came to San Francisco in reply to a telegram sent by a man you don't like, to help a girl you don't know, and you just happened to run into Sam Wing and John Chang?"

"That's what I'm asking you to believe because that's the truth. I'm not saying I wouldn't have paid those two a visit anyway, but meeting when we did was coincidence, and believe me, Kovac, I hate coincidences more than you do. As a rule, I don't believe in them, but in this case I have to make an exception."

"Yeah," Kovac said unhappily. "Look here, why didn't they just come to me when the girl disappeared."

"Do you trust them?"

"Hell, no."

"Well, they feel the same about you."

Kovac frowned.

"What do you know about the Black Pearl Tong?"

"Not a hell of a lot," the policeman admitted. "They seem to be growing quietly."

"Eventually they'll explode, Kovac, you know that. What will you do then?"

"Deal with it, as I've dealt with it before—without your help, if you can believe that."

"I'll make an effort," Clint said, standing up.

"Look, I've warned you once already. Don't go littering my city with bodies. If you find out something that I can act on, let me know."

"Sure. Are you going to look for the girl and John Chang?"

"I'll advise my men to be on the lookout. A lot of them know Wing and Chang, so they'll know who to look for."

"All right."

Clint started for the door and Kovac called out, "Adams."

"Yeah?"

"You changed hotels."

"That's right."

Kovac waited and when Clint didn't offer anything further he said, "Well, would you like to let me know where you're staying?"

Clint gave him the name of the rundown hotel on the Barbary Coast.

"What the hell are you doing there?"

"Waiting for a message. Oh, and I'm registered under a different name."

"What?"

"Archer."

Kovac frowned and said, "You didn't go through all that trouble just to avoid talking to me again, did you?"

"Like I said, I'm waiting for a message."

"Does it have something to do with Chang and the girl?"

Clint opened the door and said, "I sure as hell hope so."

Sam Wing was waiting for Clint when he left the police station.

"So?"

"Let's go somewhere and get a drink."

Wing said he knew of a place and led the way there. When they were installed at a corner table with two beers he repeated the question.

"Kovac has agreed to pass the word to his men to be on the lookout for John and Su Chow."

"He did that willingly?" Wing asked in surprise.

"I appealed to his better nature."

"I did not know he had one."

"You are obviously unaware of the high affection he has for you and John."

Wing stared at Clint in horror and said, "Do not even suggest such a thing. I am quite comfortable with the relationship just the way it is."

"Sure."

They stared into their beer for a while and then Clint broke the silence. He knew that Wing was thinking about his missing partner.

"I think we better get some sleep."

"I will go back to the office. Perhaps John will still come back there."

"Good idea," Clint said. "With a little luck, I'll see both of you tomorrow night at the office."

Clint stood up and looked down expectantly at Wing.

"I will just finish my beer and then go. You can be on your way."

Clint hesitated.

"Do not concern yourself with me, Clint," Sam Wing said. "I will be fine."

Clint wasn't all that sure, but he respected Wing too much to say so.

Clint returned to his hotel and as he entered, heard the clerk call, "Archer, hey Archer!" several times before he realized that the man was talking to him.

"Yeah?" he said, approaching the desk.

"You gotta message," the man said, holding a small slip of paper out to him.

"Thanks."

"Hey," the clerk said when Clint took the message

and made no move to give him a coin.

"Hey," Clint said, "I wouldn't want to spoil our friendship with money. Besides, you're not a post office?"

He left the man muttering and walked up to his room before reading the message. It was from Howard Clark.

Archer,

Please come to my place tomorrow afternoon to talk about possible employment.

Howard Clark

Clint folded the message and stuffed it into his pocket. Now maybe he'd be able to get somewhere.

SIXTEEN

Clint took the same precautions when he slept that night, since he was still not sure that the two men who had attacked him had come from Howard Clark. If they had, then Clark now had something else on his mind. If they hadn't, then no matter what happened with Clark, he could still be in danger—all this presupposing that the two men had not simply wanted to rob him. That would have made it a coincidence, and as he had told Kovac the night before, he didn't believe in them— unless they were forced on him.

In the morning he had a leisurely breakfast, lingering over his second pot of coffee. He decided to take Clark's invitation literally, and wait until well after twelve noon to visit him.

When he returned to the hotel after breakfast he saw a flash of white in his box. There was a different clerk on the desk so all he had to do was ask for it.

This one was from Madame Pearl, and he took it to his room to read. Similarly, she wanted Clint to come by "to talk," and asked that he come "this evening." That gave him plenty of time to hear what Howard Clark had to say.

Why would both Clark and Madame Pearl want to see him on the same day? That word that he didn't believe in popped up again, and he ignored it.

Looking for a way to pass the time before going to see Howard Clark, Clint decided to look in on Duke. San Francisco had to be the big boy's least favorite town in the country because he got very little exercise when they were there.

When he reached the livery Duke gave him a baleful stare which made him feel guilty.

"I know, big fella," he said, stroking Duke's powerful neck. "Hopefully, we won't be here too much longer."

That didn't seem to make Duke feel any better. He continued to stare.

"Maybe later on today I'll come back and take you out for a run. How would you like that?"

Duke's attitude said he'd wait and see if that really happened. Sometimes Clint thought the big horse was smarter than he was.

Actually, maybe taking him out for a run wasn't a bad idea. They could always ride out to the Biggs ranch and find something out about Jonathan's father. Maybe he could also find out something about his relationship with Lisa Lee.

"All right, big guy," he said, slapping Duke's neck, "that's what we'll do. I'll be back in a couple of hours."

He left the big animal looking totally unimpressed.

Clint arrived at the Black Pearl Saloon at one o'clock and ordered a beer from the bartender.

"Is the boss around?"

The bartender looked at him and said, "Oh yeah, I remember you."

"I've got an appointment this time. *He* wants to see

me, and don't worry, I'm still not looking for a job as a bartender.''

''I'll tell him you're here.''

''Thanks.''

When the bartender came back he told Clint to go right into Clark's office. Clint didn't think Clark would mind if he finished his beer first.

When he knocked on the door Clark's voice called out for him to come in.

''Ah, Archer,'' Clark said, getting up from behind his desk. ''Come in, have a seat. I assume you're here because you got my message.''

''That's right,'' Clint said, sitting down. ''*I* assume I'm here because you checked me out.''

Clark smiled and said, ''Would you like a brandy?''

''Sure.''

Clark poured the drink and handed it to Clint, then poured himself one and seated himself behind his desk.

''Yes, you're right, I did send a telegram to Texas to check you out,'' Clark said. ''I sent it to Labyrinth, and a few other towns.''

''And?''

''And you checked out.''

Thanks, Rick.

''What kind of a job?'' Clint asked a few moments later.

''My places gets pretty rough sometimes, Archer—by the way, do you have a first name?''

''Yes.''

When Clint did not elaborate on it Clark shrugged and continued.

''I need someone who can handle himself with his

hands and with his gun. The word I got on you is that you fit that description.''

"I do all right, but it sounds to me like all you need is a bouncer.''

"In the beginning, perhaps," Clark admitted, "but later your duties would become . . . broader.''

"After you decide whether or not you can trust me?''

"You're smart, too," Clark said. "I think you'll do fine, Archer—if you want the job.''

"Oh, I think I want the job," Clint said, "at least, for a while.''

"I guess we'll just both have to feel each other out and see how long it lasts.''

"I guess so.''

"Another drink to seal the bargain?''

"Another drink, and a little talk about money.''

He had the other drink, came to an agreement with Clark on a salary, and agreed to start work that night.

"I'll want you to start at about nine and stay until we close. Do you have any problem with that?''

"No problems at all," Clint said, meaning it more than Clark knew.

SEVENTEEN

When Clint left the Black Pearl Saloon he was pleased at how his meeting with Howard Clark had gone. He now worked at the saloon, and he'd be able to keep a close eye on Clark and determine whether or not he had any connection with the tong, or with the disappearance of Su Chow and John Chang.

His next meeting was with Madame Pearl, and although she seemed to want him to come around late, he was going to have to make it earlier so that he could get to work in the saloon by nine o'clock.

Over lunch in a small café he wished he could get in touch with Sam Wing and find out if John Chang had reappeared. He also wished he could spend the time between now and his meeting with Madame Pearl actively looking for Chang, but truth be told, he just wouldn't know where to start looking.

After lunch he went back to the livery, saddled Duke, and asked the liveryman how far out of town the Biggs spread was. The man told him it was a one hour ride north, and that gave him plenty of time to go out there and return in time to have his meeting and get back to the saloon by nine.

Just outside of town Clint gave the big, black gelding his head, and Duke sprinted away, reveling in the fact that he was finally able to stretch his legs. Clint had never seen a faster or stronger horse, had never ridden one, and he wondered now what he would do when Duke became older. The big black was now almost seven, and although he had plenty of good years left, the time would come when he had to be put out to pasture. Oh well, maybe they'd both be put out to pasture at the same time.

Who knew what the future had in store for them?

The Biggs ranch was impressive without being showy. The house was large, but there were no decorative pillars or peaks of any kind. Everything about the house was useful, and that said something about the man. He wondered how the elder Biggs felt about having such a useless son.

Clint decided that a direct frontal approach was the best, so he rode Duke right up to the front door where he was met by a tall man with an eye patch.

"Can I help you?" the man asked.

"I'd like to see Mr. Biggs."

"Mr. Biggs is busy."

"Mr. Jonathan Biggs?"

"Oh," the man said, the distaste for his employer's son plainly showing on his face. "He's out riding."

"Where?"

The man pointed and said, "Go out behind the house and up the hill. He usually rides through that field toward the hills. You'll probably catch him on his way back, now. He's got to dress for this evening."

"What's this evening?"

"He'll be going to town," the man said, "as he does every evening."

"Well, thanks a lot."

The man dismissed Clint and turned his back. Any

friend of Jonathan Biggs couldn't be worth any more than he was.

Clint took Duke behind the house and up the hill the man had mentioned. When he reached the top he could see Jonathan Biggs riding toward him, riding just the sort of horse he would have expected him to—an obvious show horse. All tail and mane, no speed and stamina. A good-looking animal with nothing underneath the looks.

Clint waited there and observed that Biggs rode very well. When the other man saw him he waved and shouted, and rode up to meet him.

"Hello," Biggs said pleasantly. "Come out for that drink?"

"I was taking my horse for a run and thought I'd stop by and take a chance that you weren't busy."

"Busy?" Biggs said, looking aghast at the prospect. "I'm never busy, Archer. Must I call you Archer? Don't you have a first name?"

"I never use it."

Biggs shrugged and said, "Well, would you like to come to the house for that drink?"

"Sure."

"You can meet my father, but be careful you don't tell him that we're friends."

"Why is that?"

"He can't stand my friends."

"Why?" Clint asked again.

Jonathan Biggs looked at Clint and said, "Well, because he thinks they're all like me, of course."

Of course.

EIGHTEEN

As they dismounted so that the man with the patch could take care of their horses Biggs said, "That's a beautiful animal."

"No," Clint said, indicating Biggs's palamino show horse, "your horse is beautiful. Duke is magnificent."

Biggs eyed Clint for a moment, then shrugged and said, "You're absolutely right." He turned to the man with the eye patch and said, "Make sure you take good care of Mr. Archer's horse, Frank, and mine, as usual."

"Right," eye patch said through clenched teeth.

As they ascended the steps to the front door Biggs said, "Don't mind Frank, he just hates me."

"Is he the foreman?"

"Yes, and I suppose he's a good one, but I've never really bothered to find out."

They went inside and Biggs said, "We'll go to my father's office. He keeps the good brandy there."

"Won't he mind?"

"Probably, but then he minds everything I do."

"It doesn't sound like you get along with your father—if you don't mind my saying so."

"I don't mind," Jonathan Biggs said. "Actually, we get along quite well because we understand each other. Now Frank, he doesn't understand me at all, so he hates me.''

"And how do you feel about him?''

"Oh, I understand Frank very well,'' Jonathan Biggs said, pouring two glasses of brandy from a glass decanter. He handed one to Clint and continued. "You see, Frank would like to be my father's son, and he can't stand the fact that he's not.''

"I can imagine,'' Clint said. "I don't think I'd be able to take a man like that lightly.''

"Oh, he'd never harm me, because he knows it would break my father's heart. Drink up, and then perhaps I can arrange for you to meet the old man.''

"I don't want to impose on him,'' Clint said. "He must be a very busy man.''

"Oh, he is,'' Jonathan assured him. "Making money is almost as hard as spending it.''

"Actually, I was curious about something other than your father,'' Clint said, deciding to be at least halfway honest.

"What's that?''

"Miss Lee.''

"Lisa? You fancy her?''

"She's very lovely.''

"She is that.''

"I was wondering about your . . . relationship. Now that we're friends I wouldn't want to, uh, get in your way or anything—''

"You'd like to take her to dinner, something like that?''

"Well, yes—''

"That would be fine,'' Jonathan said. "All you have to do is have enough money. She's very expensive.''

"Well, I think I could afford to take her someplace—"

"That's not what I meant," Jonathan Biggs said, shaking his head. "I mean *she* is expensive."

Clint couldn't believe what he was being told, and then couldn't believe that he hadn't seen it before.

"You understand, don't you?" Jonathan asked.

"Yes," Clint said, "yes, I do. She's—"

"—for hire," Biggs broke in. "That's the way I look at it. Like taking out a horse, or a buggy, from the livery stable. She's for hire, and she'll do as much as you want her to do. You can drape her over your arm for an evening's fun, or you can take her up to a hotel room."

"I see."

"It's better than going to Madame Pearl's. She gets a lot of the wrong element there."

"Uh-huh."

"Would you like me to tell you how to get in touch with her?"

"No, no, that's all right," Clint said. He was about to protest further when a large, white-haired man entered the room at full stride, and then stopped short when he saw Clint and Jonathan Biggs.

"Oh, sorry," he said gruffly. "Didn't know you had a visitor."

"Dad, I'd like you to meet Mr. Archer. We met last night at the Alhambra."

"A gambler?" the elder Biggs asked.

"It's just something I do sometimes."

"Archer, this is my father, Daniel Biggs. He's the absolute ruler of all you see."

Clint stepped forward and extended his hand, and after a moment's hesitation, the older man took it.

Daniel Biggs had to be in his mid-sixties, but his back was ramrod straight and his grip was powerful.

"Are you a friend of my son's?"

Behind Daniel Biggs the younger man frowned and shook his head.

"Like your son said, Mr. Biggs. We only just met last night. I was exercising my horse and just thought I'd stop in for a look-see. Jonathan told me you had an impressive spread, and he was right."

"You should see his horse, Dad," Jonathan said. "What a magnificent animal. Puts anything we have on the grounds to shame."

"Is that a fact?" Daniel Biggs said. "I'll have to take a look sometime, but at the moment I have some important paperwork to do." He moved toward his desk, and Clint sidestepped out of his way.

"I guess I'd better be going."

Clint had noticed that during the short time they were in the room together, Biggs, Sr., had never looked directly at Biggs, Jr. Now Jonathan walked Clint to the front door, found Frank with the eye patch, and told him to get Mr. "Archer's" horse.

"As you can see, my father usually has business on his mind," Jonathan said as they were waiting.

"I can see why."

"Really?" Jonathan asked, looking puzzled. "I can't."

That didn't surprise Clint at all.

NINETEEN

When Clint showed up at Madame Pearl's he was admitted by her man, Lee, and shown to her office. To get there, of course, they had to run the gamut and passing through all those women he spotted Chrissie, who winked at him and licked her lips.

Lee let him into Madame Pearl's office and said, "You will wait, please?"

"What else would I do?"

"You would like a girl while you wait?"

"I don't think so," Clint said. He knew why Madame Pearl kept Lee around. He was almost as good as one of those barkers on the Barbary Coast. "Maybe later."

"As you wish."

Lee left Clint by himself, and he put the time to good use by looking through Madame Pearl's desk. By the time she arrived he had satisfied himself that there was nothing in the desk to link her to the Black Pearl Tong.

"Mr. Archer," she said, gliding past him to her desk, leaving a trail of her scent.

"Madame Pearl."

"Kind of you to come, although it is a bit early."

For the first time Clint thought he might have an idea of why he had to wait for her. Had she been asleep?

"I'm sorry if I . . . took you away from something important," he said.

"Not at all," she replied serenely. "If you must know, I was sleeping. Since most of my working hours are at night, I try to sleep in the early evening hours."

"I'm sorry. I have another appointment a little later on."

"Does that mean you won't be taking advantage of my delights tonight?"

"I'm afraid not. I just have time to find out why you asked me here."

She folded her hands on the desk top and stared at him.

"Very well, then. I asked you here to offer you a job."

"A job?"

"Yes."

"Are you thinking about replacing Lee?"

"No. Your duties would be quite different from Lee's."

"How?"

"In many ways," she said, and he thought that the look she gave him was suggestive.

"Are we talking about what I think we're talking about?"

"Possibly," she said, "but there are other things, as well."

"Well, let's clear up this thing first," he said. "Do you want me around to service you in bed?"

"Would you find that distasteful?"

"Not at all, but I can't understand why a woman like you would have to pay me—"

"I own this fine establishment, Mr. Archer," she said. "I do not work here. I am also very busy. My time for recreation is very limited. I would simply like to have someone I could call upon when a certain . . . mood came upon me.''

"I see. Well, I'm very flattered—"

"The other duties," she went on, interrupting him, "would involve simply keeping the peace here."

Keeping the peace? You mean, like a lawman? Your own private lawman?''

"I did some checking on you and found that you have a reputation for being able to handle yourself. I could use a man like you around here, simply as a deterrent—"

"If we had talked about this yesterday, I might have been able to say yes."

"Why is today different from yesterday?"

"Today I have a job."

"Doing what?" she asked, looking interested.

"Just about the same thing you've asked me to do—except for one thing."

"Where?"

"The Black Pearl Saloon."

"Howard Clark's place?"

"That's right. Do you know him?"

"We've met."

"I'm sorry, but who knows. You might have been sorry you hired me—after the first time."

"I doubt that."

"Why?"

A smile touched her lips, although it didn't quite make it to her almond-shaped eyes, and she said, "Intuition."

Sure, he thought, intuition and watching him with Little Chrissie.

"How good is your intuition?"

Now the smile spread to her eyes and she said, "We could always put it to the test—if you have the time, that is."

"Are you asking me—I mean, like with Little Chrissie—"

"No, not like with Chrissie," Madame Pearl said. "Upstairs, in my room."

"Isn't this a little unusual?"

"What do you mean?"

"I mean, for a woman like you to ask a man to—"

"You are a very unusual man, Mr. Archer. You are right, however, it is an unusual offer, but it is one that I will only make once."

They regarded each other silently for some time and then Clint said, "If I say yes, it won't mean I'm taking the job. I mean, I've already accepted Howard Clark's offer."

"Without hearing mine?" she asked. "Is that fair?"

"He did make his first."

"Come upstairs with me," she said, "and perhaps I can make mine more . . . attractive."

"All right," he said after a moment, "but this will set some sort of record, won't it?"

She stood up and asked, "What do you mean?"

"I mean, the same man getting two free samples from the same whorehouse?"

"It is not a whorehouse," she said, taking his arm, "it is a Palace of Delight."

Clint noticed that as they walked back through the room full of girls with Madame Pearl holding onto his arm, none of the girls looked at him. He went so far as to make a point of looking at Chrissie, but instead of winking and licking her lips she found something interesting about the ceiling at that moment. He assumed that her arm through his was the sign that he was not available—at least not tonight.

TWENTY

Madame Pearl's room was ostentatious, to say the least, but that was no surprise. The whole establishment mirrored the madame's expensive tastes.

"Are all the rooms this fancy?" he asked.

"To a lesser degree, yes," she said. "Not quite this large, but the furnishings are lovely."

The bed was unmade attesting to the fact that she'd been in it when he had arrived. It looked somehow warm and inviting in its untidy state.

Madame Pearl was wearing a kimono-type garment, tied at the waist. Now she pulled at it, loosening it so that it gaped open. Beneath it she was naked, and invitingly so. The view of her breasts revealed them to be full and firm, well-rounded, tipped with dark brown nipples. In her own way she was every bit as lovely as Lisa Lee had been, although the younger woman had a presence that most women only dreamed about having.

"Would you like me to have the sheets changed?" she asked, indicating the rumpled bed.

"No, I don't see any problem with these," he replied. "You, uh, were alone in bed, I presume."

"I was," she said, shrugging the kimono from her shoulders to the floor, "but no longer."

Sometime later she said, "You see?"

"What?"

"My intuition was correct."

"I'm glad you feel that way."

"I am pleased, also, to find that I was correct," she said, placing her hand over his stomach. "You are in excellent shape for a man your age."

"Well, thanks."

"Age is a state of mind," she informed him, laughing gently. "Look at me. How old would you say I am?"

He considered his answer very carefully. It was becoming obvious that she took great pride in her appearance and her condition, which would naturally add years to his original estimate. Yet tact dictated he subtract a few years rather than add them.

"Oh, I don't know," he said. "Mid-to late-thirties, I suppose."

"You see?" she said, obviously pleased. "I am over forty, yet I do not appear to be so."

"Very impressive."

She regarded him for a moment, then laughed again and said, "Forgive me my vanity, Archer. It *is* my only vice."

"I doubt that."

She sat up in bed, presenting him with a view of her gracefully curved back.

"What do you say to the job, then?"

"I told you before, I have a job."

"But surely this position is much more attractive than his. Don't tell me you have principles? A man like you?"

"What kind of a man am I?"

She looked at him over her lovely shoulder and said, "Don't be offended. I checked you out, Mr. Archer—I feel odd sitting with you in my bed, calling you Mister.

Don't you have a first name?"

"Archer will do," he said. "Just drop the 'Mister' and call me Archer."

"Very well. . . . Archer. I checked you out, you know. You seem to have quite a reputation in Texas."

"I've been there."

"To say the least. You have a reputation as a man proficient with a gun—deadly, as a matter of fact."

"Is that so?"

"Yes. I believe I can use you, Archer—in more ways than one. Think about my offer. Work for Howard Clark for a while and think it over."

She got up and he admired the high, round cheeks of her behind as she slid back into the kimono.

"I'm afraid I have a business to run. Will you be staying?"

"I'm afraid I have a job to go to," he said, getting out of bed.

She walked to the door and said, "Please close the door behind you when you leave. I'll look forward to hearing from you soon.'

"I'll be in touch."

When she left he sat at the edge of the bed, drumming his bare feet on the floor, wondering how she had known to check him out in Texas. He'd never told her what hotel he was staying in, and that just was one of the two places she would have been able to find out the address he was using.

The other way she could have found out was from Howard Clark.

TWENTY-ONE

When Clint got to the Black Pearl Saloon the place was going strong, packed wall-to-wall. There were a few gaming tables spread about, but for the most part Howard Clark seemed to feel that people would prefer to gamble among themselves, instead of trying to buck a house game.

Clint presented himself at the bar and told the bartender, "Tell the boss I'm here, will you?"

"Sure."

"Before you go—do employees drink on the house?"

"Long as they don't drink us dry."

"Then let me have a beer, will you?"

The man drew him a beer and then went to tell Clark that he was there. When he returned he just nodded to Clint, and since there were no special instructions forthcoming he decided that all he had to do was stand around and keep his eyes open—which was just what he wanted to do, anyway. If the saloon was a base of operations for the tong, there was sure to be some activity to indicate such.

One drawback of this job was that he'd have to wait until the Black Pearl closed before he could go to meet with Wing at his office. He hoped that Wing would wait for him.

As the night progressed, Clint was called upon once or twice to mediate an argument. He resolved one by calming both parties, and the other by evicting both parties so they could carry on their disagreement in the street without danger of disturbing anyone or busting up any furniture.

It was about two in the morning before something interesting developed. Clint was sitting at an out of the way table watching over the place when a man walked in, stopped just inside the front batwing doors, and then walked across the crowded room directly to the door of Howard Clark's office. What was even more interesting was that along the way he exchanged nods with the bartender, and then entered the office without bothering to knock.

The most interesting thing of all, however, was the fact that Clint recognized the man. The identification was made all the more easier by the man's eye patch.

It was Frank, the ramrod at the Biggs ranch.

Clint waited to see when Frank would come out, but by the time the saloon was ready to close the man still had not reappeared. Finally, as the last patron was being ushered out, the door opened, and Howard Clark came out.

"Well, how was your first night?" he asked Clint.

"Not too bad," Clint said, telling him about the two disagreements he'd refereed.

"Well, you can leave now. In fact, you can leave every night right after the last customer does."

"All right."

"Wait."

Clint stopped, and Clark reached into his pocket and came up with a wad of money.

"Here's your first week in advance. Why don't you get yourself a better place to stay?"

"I'll do that," Clint said. He debated mentioning the man with the patch to Clark, then decided against it. "See you tomorrow, then."

"Good night."

Clint left the saloon, and Clark closed the doors securely behind him. He crossed the street and started to position himself in a doorway to wait, then cursed himself for a fool. Of course Frank had probably used the rear door to leave. He was long gone by now, but it was enough that Clint had seen him. Could the man's presence suggest a connection between Daniel Biggs—or Jonathan Biggs?

Maybe he should find Jonathan and ask him.

TWENTY-TWO

Clint went to Sam Wing's office and, after using his key to get in, found the detective lying on the couch.

"Asleep?"

"No," Wing said, swinging his feet to the floor. "Just waiting."

"For me?"

"Or John."

"You haven't heard from him?"

"Not a peep."

Wing stood up, walked to the desk and poured himself a drink from a bottle that was almost empty. That was odd, because Clint was used to seeing Wing drinking his *soochong* tea.

"You go through that?"

Wing looked up with the bottle in his hand, then looked at the bottle and said, "No. It was left over from John. Actually, I don't really want it," he said, and put the bottle and glass back down. "How was your day?"

"I got a job," Clint said, "and a job offer." He explained everything to Wing, including the man with the patch at the Black Pearl Saloon.

"Why are these people suddenly so anxious to offer you a job?" Wing asked.

"To keep an eye on me?"

"Why should they want to do that? You've done

nothing to make them suspicious of you."

"Maybe they're just naturally suspicious of everyone," Clint suggested.

Wing sat wearily behind his desk and said, "Are you suggesting a connection in all this with Daniel Biggs?"

"What do you know about Biggs?"

Wing rubbed his face with both hands, pausing to dig his thumbs into his eyes, and then said, "He's got a lot of land, a lot of stock, and a lot of influence in the state."

"He's also got a son who likes to gamble his money away. I assume he's also got a lot of money?"

"So far, but at the rate his son is going, it won't last much longer. How did you know about the son?"

"I met him the other night," Clint said, and explained the circumstances. He did not mention Lisa Lee. It didn't seem necessary.

"You know what you're talking about here, don't you?" Sam Wing asked.

"Yes," Clint said, nodding, "I do." He made a face and said, "Coincidence."

"Your meeting with Jonathan Biggs could not possibly have been planned, could it?"

"No. I didn't even know I'd be at the Alhambra that night until moments before. Much as I hate to admit it, it had to be coincidental."

"What about this man with the patch? Frank?"

"Maybe you could find out something about him tomorrow."

"I could try, but I had intended to look for John tomorrow."

Clint studied Wing's worried face and then said, "Okay, you look for John, and I'll check out my friend with the patch."

"How will you do that?"

"I'll ask Jonathan, or better yet, I'll ask Frank himself. What could be easier than that?"

TWENTY-THREE

The next morning after breakfast Duke got to stretch his legs again. Clint saddled him and rode out to the Biggs ranch. This time, as he rode up to the front door, there was a different man there to meet him and ask him his business.

"Is Frank around?"

"Frank?"

"The foreman. I don't know his last name. A man with a patch?"

"Fletcher, you mean Frank Fletcher."

"That's the man."

"I guess he's around somewhere. Can't tell you exact, though."

"What about Mr. Biggs, Jonathan Biggs?"

"In the house, I reckon."

"Would you take care of my horse? I won't be long."

"Sure."

Clint went up the steps to the front door and knocked loudly. It was answered by the very man he was looking for, Jonathan Biggs.

"Archer."

"Hello, Jonathan. Can we talk for a few minutes?"

"Sure, sure. Come on in. I'll get you a drink."

They settled down in the living room, rather than in

the elder Biggs's office, and Jonathan asked, "What is this all about? Not Lisa Lee again?"

"No, it's about your father's foreman, Frank Fletcher."

"What about him?"

"What do you know about him?"

"Not much. He's been with my father for about twelve years. I was away when he first started working here, and when I returned he seemed to instantly resent my presence."

"And you've been putting up with each other all this time?"

"Ten years."

"A man can build up a lot of hate in ten years."

"Him, or me?"

Clint shrugged.

"Why are you interested in Frank Fletcher?"

"Just something I saw last night."

"What?"

Clint told Jonathan that he was working in the Black Pearl Saloon and saw Frank walk in like he owned the place.

"Maybe he's been saving his money all these years? Maybe he owns a piece of it? So what?"

How much could Clint tell Jonathan? That he was looking into the existence of something called the Black Pearl Tong and was now wondering if his father was involved with it?

"I was just curious," he finally said, "and looking for another excuse to let my horse stretch his legs."

"Hey, speaking about your horse, you wouldn't want to race him, would you? Against mine? For a little wager?"

"I'm afraid not."

"Why not? Afraid he'll get beat?"

"I know he can't be beat," Clint said, "so I've got nothing to prove, and neither does he."

"Well, if you change your mind—"

"I won't. Do you know where Fletcher is right now?"

"Probably checking the stock. If you want to stretch your horse's legs a little more, you might try the north pasture."

"I'll do that."

"Will you be in Portsmouth Square tonight?"

"I doubt it."

"I'll have Lisa with me."

Clint paused, then said, "Give her my regards, will you?"

"Sure. Come by, and I'll get you two together. I don't know exactly which place we'll be in, but we won't be hard to find."

"If I'm in the area—" Clint said, and let it lie at that.

Jonathan walked him to the front door and told the man outside to get Clint's horse.

"See you this evening, perhaps."

"Perhaps," Clint said. He mounted up and directed Duke toward the north pasture, hoping to find Frank Fletcher.

There were several men in the pasture, among the cattle, but the man with the eye patch was not hard to pick out, and Clint rode toward him.

"Hello," he called.

Fletcher looked up from the ground, where he was crouched over a calf, frowned, and ignored Clint.

Clint dismounted and walked over to the man.

"You want something?" the man finally asked

when Clint stood staring at him.

"Just some conversation."

Fletcher stood up and faced Clint squarely.

"I got nothing to say to you."

"Why is that? You got something to hide?"

"I got nothing to hide, and nothing to say, especially not to any friend of that—Oh, hell. Get out of my way!"

Fletcher put his hand on Clint's shoulder to push him out of the way, but as he pushed Clint stepped back to avoid the pressure. As he did so, the other man stumbled and fell.

"Why you—" he said, leaping to his feet.

"Sorry about that, Fletcher, but I don't like being pushed."

"I'll do a lot worse than push you—"

"Wouldn't it be easier just to talk to me?" Clint suggested.

The man glared at Clint, his jaw thrust out belligerently, and then said, "What about?"

"The Black Pearl Saloon."

"What about it?" Fletcher asked, his one eye narrowing.

"You were there last night."

"So?"

"Would you mind telling me why?"

"Why I was there? Why would I want to tell you that? And why would you want to know? What's going on?"

"I'm just curious. Why don't you humor me?"

"I don't know why I should. I went to a saloon for a drink, so what?"

"At two in the morning? And you didn't stop at the

bar, you went right to Howard Clark's office and entered without knocking.''

"I don't know what you're talking about."

"I guess you and Clark are just friends, huh?''

"I don't know anyone by that name, friend. I've got work to do, and I can't stand here talking to you all day. Do you mind?''

"No, I don't mind at all.''

Clint walked back to Duke and mounted up. Fletcher mounted his horse and rode off toward the herd.

At least Clint had found out something. Fletcher obviously knew Howard Clark, yet denied it. There was definitely a connection between Clark and Fletcher, but was Clark connected with the tong and if so, what was Fletcher's part?

Well, he'd probably find something out that night. By the time he showed up for work, Fletcher was sure to have spoken to Clark about Clint's questions. All that remained was to see what Clark's reaction would be.

Fletcher left Clint and went right to the leader of the Black Pearl Tong. He told him about the encounter with the man he knew as ''Archer''.

"You're a fool,'' the man told him, ''and so is Clark. What the hell were you doing at the saloon anyway?''

"Well, I—''

"Even if you had to go there you should have used the back door.''

"How was I supposed to know Archer was there? What's he asking questions for, anyway?''

"Maybe he was just curious. It was his first day on

the job and he was keeping his eyes open," the other man suggested, but he didn't really believe that. "You better go and let Clark know about this, Fletcher."

"Yes, sir," Fletcher said, starting for the door.

"And for God's sake use the back door!"

After Fletcher left, the tong leader poured himself a drink and thought about this man Archer. First he meets Jonathan Biggs, then he ends up working for Howard Clark. What was he after?

Clark had checked him out before hiring him, but maybe Mr. Archer required a little more extensive looking into.

The tong leader decided that, whatever there was to know about the man, he'd know before the day was out, and if he wasn't what he was pretending to be, he was as good as dead.

Clark reacted calmly to Fletcher's news, even though he knew that the tong leader was not pleased.

"You're a fool, Fletcher."

Fletcher became angry.

"I don't have to take that from you, Clark—"

"Why not? You're the one who came into my place by the front door, bold as you please, and you're the one who was stupid enough to deny knowing me. Christ, man, Archer told you he saw you, how could you say that?"

"I—I didn't know what to say—" Fletcher stammered. "I didn't expect anybody to ask me no questions."

"That's obvious. All right, at least we've got Archer where we can keep an eye on him while we check him further. Go back and tell the leader not to worry. I'll handle it."

"I got the feeling that the leader was going to handle it himself, Clark."

Clark cursed inwardly. He couldn't afford to have the leader think that he wasn't capable of handling things himself.

"You tell him not to worry, you hear? I'll find out just what Archer is after, and I'll take care of him myself."

"Sure," Fletcher said, standing up.

"And use the back door!"

Fletcher frowned and couldn't help thinking that worse things could happen than having Clark fall flat on his face in front of the old man.

"Good luck," he told Clark, but he didn't mean a word of it.

TWENTY-FOUR

Clint was disappointed.

He had gone to work that night expecting Clark to call him in to speak to him, but he did not see Howard Clark all night, and when the time came to close, he debated between leaving and forcing a confrontation. He decided then that he'd done enough to force one and simply had to wait for it to come.

He discussed the day's events with Sam Wing in his office later that night.

"Well, at least you got the man Fletcher to give you some damaging information."

"That he didn't know Clark, yes. I agree. He obviously wanted to hide the connection between the two of them."

"This is all very interesting," Sam Wing said. "We've established a connection between Howard Clark and someone on the Biggs ranch, but we have not yet been able to establish any connection between Clark's Black Pearl Saloon and the Black Pearl Tong. That's what we need, Clint."

"I know. Did you have any luck at all today in trying to track John down?"

"None."

Something occurred to Clint then, and he decided to see how Sam Wing felt about it.

123

"Sam, how good a detective is John?"

"John is an excellent detective."

"As good as you? Or better?"

Wing hesitated, then said, "Every bit as good, I would say. In some ways, better, and in other ways I am better."

"Sam, what if John didn't want to be found?"

Wing frowned and said, "What do you mean?"

"I mean just that. What if he was staying out of sight for some reason of his own. What if he didn't want you to find him? Could you?"

"I do not know," Wing said carefully.

"But if that were the case," Clint went on, "would you change your tactics for finding him?"

"Significantly."

"Then why don't you do that?"

"I don't understand why you think John would deliberately drop out of sight—"

"I'm not saying he has, but what could it hurt for you to change your tactics?"

Wing thought a moment then shrugged and said, "None."

"Then you'll do it?"

"I suppose so."

"Just try and figure out where he'd be if he didn't want to be found?"

"There are a lot of places, a lot of friends we have in common who might help him."

"Maybe John is hoping that his absence will make somebody nervous, force somebody to make a move they don't really want to make?"

"It is possible," Wing said, "but why would he do this without confiding in me?"

"I don't know, Sam, but if that is the case, you

could always ask him—once you find him.''

Wing actually looked as if he had suddenly become more awake, more alert. The idea was starting to appeal to him.

''This might be something John would do.''

''Then now's the time to find out who the better detective is, Sam. Find him.''

''I will find him,'' Sam Wing said, ''and if what you say is true, Clint, I may need your help.''

''To do what?''

Wing stood up behind his desk and said with feeling, ''To keep me from killing him.''

Clint left Sam Wing seated behind his desk, considering the new course of action he'd suggested. On the way back to his hotel—and it would be his last night in that dump, he'd decided—he went over his present situation.

He had set himself up right inside the jaws of the tiger by taking the job with Clark at the Black Pearl, but now who was keeping an eye on who? He was sure that Frank Fletcher would report their conversation to Howard Clark—in fact, must have already done so. Clark was obviously still considering his options, because he had taken no action that night. There was nothing for Clint to do but wait.

What about Madame Pearl? Of course he didn't buy the story about wanting him on call as a bed partner. She wanted him around also to keep an eye on him, and he wouldn't have minded staying around to keep an eye open as well, but he had to decide where his best chance of finding a connection with the tong was, at the saloon or at Madame Pearl's ''Palace of Delight.''

As far as he was concerned, his choice had to be the

saloon. He simply felt that with the name being the same as the tong and with Fletcher's appearance, the saloon was where his best opportunity lay. He'd made his choice, and now he'd have to live it.

He just hoped he wouldn't die with it, instead.

As Clint Adams walked through the darkened streets of Chinatown, wending his way back to the Barbary Coast, he was unaware of the darkly clothed man who was following him. His failure to be aware of the man was not due to any carelessness on his part, but rather to the ability of the man who was following him. The man, tall, slim and lithe, seemed to blend in with the shadows like a ghost. Even if the Gunsmith had suddenly turned and stared behind, he would have failed to see him.

Such was the skill of the dark man that Clint Adams would not become aware of his presence until the man allowed him to.

TWENTY-FIVE

The next morning before going to breakfast Mr. "Archer" checked out of his hotel and into a slightly better establishment on Market Street. It wasn't the Alhambra, but it was a lot more sanitary than the place he'd spent his last few nights—*and* it had a dining room, which he tried immediately and found palatable.

While Clint Adams was having his breakfast, there was a man in a telegraph office near Portsmouth Square sending out telegrams concerning a man who fit the Gunsmith's description. The man was not sending a name with the description, but was simply asking some friends of his if they could match a name to the man. The man, who was a respected citizen of San Francisco, preferred to assume that the name "Archer" was an alias and was confident that his telegrams would reap a harvest of several names, which he would use to try to discover his true identity.

"Please have any replies brought to my house immediately," the man said to the clerk, paying him and adding something extra.

The clerk looked at the amount of money that was in his hand, did some quick subtraction, then said to the man's retreating back, "Yes, sir!"

Howard Clark, at that moment, was in another telegraph office, near the Barbary Coast, sending some telegrams of his own. His messages were going to different people—indeed, a different class of people—but the questions were the same, as was the method. He ignored the name "Archer" and simply asked that a name be matched with his description.

Clark left the telegraph office telling himself that he had hired the man, so now he had to show the tong leader that he could correct his own mistakes *without* extensive damage being done by the blunder.

Perhaps the best would have been to simply to have "Archer" killed, but he decided to first try and find out the man's real name, and why he was in San Francisco.

And so much for Clark's "need" for a right-hand man. He would just have to accept his position as the tong leader's right-hand man, and let it go at that. Try to pretend you're something that you're not, and you end up making a fool of yourself.

He did not intend that to happen again, and he intended the man who had brought it about to pay for it—dearly!

Madame Pearl stood before a full-length mirror in her bedroom, naked, admiring the thrust of her breasts. She took pride in the fact that she had the body of a woman fifteen years younger than she was. She ran her hands over her stomach, and her face registered satisfaction.

Dressing for bed her thoughts turned to the man she knew as "Archer." She had heard from Howard Clark about Archer's conversation with Fletcher, and she agreed that the man had to be more than he seemed. She had also argued with Clark because he had not told her that he intended to offer Archer a job, and she had not told him of her plans to do the same. They were both trying to set the man up so that they could keep an eye on him, but they should have consulted one another before putting it into practice. Even if the man had not suspected a connection between Clark and Madame Pearl, the coincidence of two job offers in one day would surely make him think.

She sighed as she slid between the sheets. Perhaps she'd get a chance to find out who she had really been to bed with the other night before he died.

Sam Wing woke up that morning and immediately tried to put himself in John Chang's shoes. If he himself did not wish to be seen, where would he go?

His partner John Chang had a complex mind, but Wing vowed that he would figure it out and find him.

He was not even thinking about Su Chow anymore. His partner's safety took precedence in his mind over the safety of a girl who, truth be told, he did not even like and was probably even a little jealous of.

Wing stepped out of his office, paused in front of the door, and thought, Where are you, John? I hope to God that wherever you are you're there because you want to be.

Chief Inspector Kovac was incensed.

"What do you mean they lost them?" he asked the young policeman standing in front of his desk.

"I'm sorry, sir. The man we had following Clint Adams said that he just lost him, but the man we had following the detective, Sam Wing, says that *Wing* lost *him*."

"And now I have no idea where either man is or what the hell they're doing."

"Uh, no sir."

"Because my men are incompetent."

"No sir—I mean, yes sir—I mean—"

"Get out, Martin."

"Sir?"

"I want you to get out there and find those men."

"Me, sir? Find . . . both of them? Alone?"

Kovac closed his eyes and said, "Use your imagination, Martin. Take the men you need and find those two for me—today!"

"Yes, sir."

As much as Kovac hated to consider it, he thought that maybe he ought to offer both Adams and Wing—and the other one, Chang—a position on his police force—if his men ever found them!

TWENTY-SIX

When Clint Adams walked into Kovac's office the Chief Inspector registered surprise on his face, without attempting to disguise it.

"Well, I didn't expect to see you here."

"Why not?" Clint asked innocently. "Didn't you ask me to keep in touch?"

"That I did, but who expected you to listen?"

"See, that's your problem, Inspector. You don't trust people."

"I'll work on it. You know you lost one of my men today."

"It wasn't intentional, I assure you," Clint said, taking a seat. "I didn't even know he was there. All I did was leave my hotel, have breakfast and then come here."

"That's all?"

"Well, there was one other thing, but that's what I came here to tell you about."

"And what's that?"

"I've changed hotels."

"That's what you came here to tell me?"

"And if I really wanted to avoid you, I wouldn't be here telling you this, would I?"

"I'll grant you that," Kovac said. "Now, my question is: Why?"

"To cooperate."

Kovac frowned and took down the name of the Gunsmith's new hotel.

"What name this time?"

"Archer," Clint said, as if it was obvious.

"Archer," Kovac repeated, writing it down.

"Have you come up with anything on John Chang?"

"Nothing," Kovac said, putting down his pencil, "but then my men lost both of you, and apparently you weren't trying to lose him. I don't know about Wing."

"You're saying you don't have much confidence in your men's abilities to find Chang?"

"I'm saying—" Kovac began and then stopped short. He started again in a softer tone. "I'm saying that I'm doing the best I can with what I've got."

"I see."

"What have you come up with?"

"Some new questions."

"Such as."

"What do you know about Daniel Biggs and his son, Jonathan?"

"Biggs is a respected businessman, and he knows how to make money. His son, on the other hand, only knows how to spend it, but he seems to do it quite well." Suddenly Kovac's eyes narrowed and he demanded, "What's your interest in Biggs?"

"Curiosity," Clint said, shrugging the question off. "I met Jonathan in Portsmouth Square, and we got to talking. I also stopped by his father's spread while I was exercising my horse."

"You met the old man, too?"

"Yes."

Kovac didn't like that. Biggs was a big man in San Francisco, and Kovac didn't need him complaining to him about being bothered.

"I'd better not hear from Mr. Biggs that you been bothering him."

"*Mister* Biggs? Does he get some kind of special treatment from your police department, Inspector."

Kovac frowned and said, "Nobody gets special treatment, Adams, but I won't have our leading citizens being harassed. Do you have some reason to believe that Biggs is involved with the Black Pearl Tong?"

"No," Clint answered honestly. All he knew was that Biggs's ramrod was involved with the owner of the Black Pearl Saloon. Beyond that he had only his own suspicions, and he wasn't about to voice them to the Inspector.

"Well," Clint said, standing up, "I've told you what I came to tell you."

"You changed hotels again. How many times are you going to do that?"

Clint shrugged and said, "Maybe until I find one I like, who knows?"

The Gunsmith started for the door, then stopped and turned to ask, "Would you like me to take it easy on the next man you assign to follow me?"

"As long as you continue to show me that you're cooperating and not causing trouble, I don't think there'll be any reason to have you followed."

"Oh? Well, that's a relief."

"Just make sure you keep cooperating," Kovac reminded him.

"Oh, I will, Inspector. I promise."

Clint's tone was so overly innocent that Kovac growled, "Get your butt out of here before I change my mind."

"Whatever you say, Inspector," Clint said and left.

Outside, in front of the police station, Clint thought about his real reason for visiting Kovac and informing him of his change of hotels. He really didn't need to have Kovac and his men on his mind, and he was getting tired of losing the men the Inspector sent to follow him. The last one had been a little more difficult because he'd wanted to do it without *seeming* to. By letting Kovac think he was cooperating, the Inspector might relax a little and give Clint more breathing room. He especially didn't want any policemen showing up at the Black Pearl Saloon. Things were going to get tense enough there as it was.

Having someone at the saloon to back him up might be a good idea, and he figured to talk to Wing about that later on that night. He'd do this one more night at the saloon alone, and then try to arrange for Wing— maybe in some kind of disguise—to be there with him until this thing finally broke.

And it had to break soon. *If* Clark was indeed connected with the tong, then having Clint around would not seem like such a good idea anymore. A move would have to be made, and Clint would feel better having Wing there to back him up when it came.

Sam Wing spend a good portion of the day checking with contacts that both he and John Chang had. He checked "safe houses" that they had both set up, where they could drop out of sight for a while if the need arose. He even checked with Amanda Lincoln, who had not seen John for days.

It was only after Sam Wing went back to the office he shared with Chang and prepared himself a cup of *soochong* tea that he paused to use his imagination to put himself in John Chang's place.

If his partner did indeed *want* to stay out of sight, what would his purpose be? How would John put his disappearance to good use?

"That is it," he said finally, smacking the desk top with his hand, spilling his tea.

Wing stood up, ignoring the tea that had slopped onto the desk, and left to try and find the Gunsmith. He had the answer, and he was too impatient to wait until late that evening.

Once again Clint Adams did not see the man who was following him, even now in broad daylight. Although there were no shadows for him to use, the man had the skill to blend with his surroundings. Several times the Gunsmith actually *did* look behind him but did not find the man who was following him—again through no carelessness of his own.

The man followed the Gunsmith for the remainder of the day, until Clint Adams went to the Black Pearl Saloon for his night's work. At this time the man took up position outside the saloon, waiting for the proper moment for him to enter, blending in with the crowd.

He would not be noticed unless he wanted to be.

To a certain degree Clint felt safe within the confines of the Black Pearl Saloon. Surely Howard Clark would not try anything violent inside his own establishment. That would call undue notice to the place, and even if the man *wasn't* involved with the tong, he wouldn't want that.

Still, if Howard paid a couple of hardcases to pick a fight with him there was always the possibility that it would end up out in the street, where anything could happen.

If he let it.

The Gunsmith had not lived this long by allowing other people to control his life.

Howard Clark cracked open the door to his office so that he could look out and check on the man he still knew as Archer. He had not gotten any answers to his telegrams yet, which disturbed him, but he would certainly have his answers early the next day. Let the man enjoy his last night of work.

The tong leader, on the other hand, had some answers. He had three names and one of them had to belong to the man who was calling himself "Archer".

He could have been Warren Murphy, the Irish Gun, who was a tall man who could handle a gun, but Murphy was said to be in the New Mexico Territory.

He could have been a gunman known as Fred Hammer, who was also tall and had a reputation with a gun, but Hammer was a black man, so that ruled him out.

That left one name: Clint Adams, otherwise known as the Gunsmith. If that was the case, then it would take someone equally as good with a gun to take care of him, and make it look as if the man's reputation had gotten him killed. There would be no link with the tong, at all.

A gunman named Long Taylor was on his way to San Francisco to take care of this little matter. Luckily,

Taylor had been nearby in Santa Rosa and would be in San Francisco by morning.

By afternoon, Clint Adams would no longer be a problem, and business could continue as usual.

TWENTY-SEVEN

When Sam Wing walked into the Black Pearl Saloon two men reacted. Clint Adams stared at him in surprise as he walked to the bar and ordered a drink.

Neither Wing nor Clint saw the tall man leave the saloon just moments after Wing had entered.

Later, at Wing and Chang's office, Sam Wing explained it to Clint.

"I was there looking for John."

"What made you think he would be there?"

"If John is missing by choice, I cannot believe that he would simply put his head in the ground and stay there. He would still want to know what was going on."

"By hanging around the Black Pearl Saloon?"

"No," Wing said, shaking his head. "By following you."

"Following—you mean John's been following me all this time, and I haven't seen him?" Clint asked in disbelief.

"You wouldn't," Wing said, "and don't feel bad that you have not. That is John's specialty. He can blend with the shadows at night and with his surroundings by day. I think he was in that saloon, but he was so well-disguised that even I did not recognize him.

Either that, or he left just before or as soon as I entered.''

"Wait a minute,'' Clint said, holding up one hand. "Wait—I think I remember a man leaving the saloon just after you entered.''

"What did he look like?''

Clint thought for a moment, trying to concentrate, but he just could not bring the man to mind.

"I don't know.''

Wing smiled and said, "That was John.''

TWENTY-EIGHT

Late the night before, after Clark had closed the saloon, Fletcher had shown up at the rear door. It was then that Clark found out that "Archer" was probably Clint Adams, the Gunsmith, and that Long Taylor was due in town to take care of him.

"Is this fella Taylor that good?" he asked Fletcher.

"I don't know," the man with the patch said. "You'll be the first to know, though, because he's gonna report to you. The old man wants you to handle it."

"That makes sense," Clark said, and he didn't see the disgusted look on Frank Fletcher's face.

The first thing Howard Clark noticed about Long Taylor was his eyes. They chilled him. It was like looking into the eyes of a dead man.

"You're Clark?"

"That's right," the saloon owner said. "You'll be taking your orders from me."

Long Taylor was so named because of his long face. He smiled grimly now, lengthening his face even more, and said, "I don't take orders from anyone. You're gonna show me who you want dead, and then you're gonna pay me after he's dead. That's all."

"I see."

"Good. So who do you want dead?"

"A man who may or may not be the Gunsmith."
Clark studied Taylor's impassive face and said, "Do
you know who he is?"

"Don't be a horse's ass, friend," Taylor said in
disgust, "of course I know who he is. I'll also be able
to tell you whether or not your man is Adams. I've seen
him."

"Can you take him?"

"I can take anybody—but the price has gone up."

"What?"

"I didn't know about Adams. If it is him, the price is
double."

"I can't—"

"Yeah, I know, you can't okay that. Well, you just
talk to the man who can and then let me know. I'll be
staying at the hotel nearest to here."

"All the hotels around here are filthy."

"That's all right, I don't plan on doing any
entertaining—at least, not until after the job is done."

Taylor moved away from the desk to the front door
of Clark's office and from there said, "Check with
your boss, friend, and let me know. If I don't hear from
you by tonight, I'm gone in the morning."

"You'll hear from me."

Long Taylor shrugged, as if it really made no difference to him if he did or didn't, and left.

Long Taylor was back in Clark's office a few hours
later.

"The price is approved."

"Good," Taylor said.

"We have other problems, though."

"Who?"

"Two detectives."

"Pinks?"

"No, they're not Pinkertons. They're two indepen-
dents, and they're both Oriental."

"You want them dead, too?"

"I do."

"What are their names?"

"Sam Wing and John Chang."

"It'll cost extra for the chinks."

"That's approved, also."

"Where do I find them?"

"Well, Sam Wing is around, but his partner, John
Chang, seems to have disappeared."

"Your people have anything to do with that?"

"That's just it," Clark said, "we didn't touch him.
He seems to have gone to ground himself."

"Did you ever think that maybe he left town?" Long
Taylor suggested.

"I doubt that. Neither one of those Chinamen would
do that. They're too stubborn."

"They sound like my kind of chinks," Taylor said.
"Maybe they'll even put up a little fight, huh?"

"After you've taken care of Adams, we'll show you
where Wing is. Before you kill him you might per-
suade him to tell you where his partner is."

"It'll be a pleasure," Long Taylor said. "I can't
stand chinks—except for their women, of course. You
got a lot of slant-eyed women in ths town, don't you?"

"There are plenty."

"Yeah. I'll have to look into that—after the job is
over."

"When will that be?" Clark asked.

"Where will this fella be, the one you think is the
Gunsmith?"

"He'll be here, tonight, but I don't want him killed in my place."

"How do you know he'll be here?"

Clark laughed ironically and said, "He works here."

"That's cozy."

"I didn't know who he was when I hired him. He's spying on us—on me—"

"Well, after tonight he won't be spying on anyone—no matter who he is," Long Taylor said. "You can take that to the bank."

Clark hoped that the man was right.

TWENTY-NINE

"He's broken it off," Sam Wing said.

They were in a café sharing a pot of coffee, after having unsuccessfully tried to flush out John Chang. They had decided that Clint would walk through Chinatown, as if he had a definite destination in mind, and Sam Wing would trail behind, trying to spot Chang.

"Maybe you just haven't been able to spot him?" Clint suggested.

Wing gave Clint a scornful look and said, "He's my partner, Clint. Now that I know what he's up to, I'll be able to spot him, but he's got to be there." Sam Wing was very definite when he said, "He's just not there, now."

"What's he got in mind, Sam?"

"Forcing somebody's hand, maybe. If we don't know where he is, neither do they. That might make them nervous enough to do something stupid."

"I have a feeling this thing might come to a head tonight," Clint said.

"At the saloon?"

"Yes. I think maybe you'd better be there to back me up."

"Don't worry, Clint," Sam Wing said. "I'll be there. In fact, I think I speak for John when I say we will both be there, I think I can speak for John when I say we will both be there."

THIRTY

When Clint got to the Black Pearl Saloon that night he didn't see Sam Wing or John Chang, but he knew that didn't mean that neither one was there.

He went to the bar and the bartender automatically handed him a beer, which he took to a back table with him. He sat down and ran his eyes over the crowd, trying to figure out which man could have been either Wing or Chang in disguise.

The door to Howard Clark's office opened a crack, and a pair of eyes looked out, found the man called "Archer," and examined him, and then the door closed.

"Yeah," Long Taylor said, turning to face Howard Clark, "that's Clint Adams, all right. That's the Gunsmith."

"Damn," Clark said with feeling. The fact that Archer *did* turn out to be the Gunsmith just made him look worse in front of the leader. "I want him dead, Taylor, and I want him dead tonight."

"That's what you're paying for."

Taylor turned, walked to the door and through it into the saloon.

Clint Adams saw the man come out of Clark's of-

147

fice, walk to the bar, and order a drink. When the man turned with drink in hand and surveyed the room, Clint thought he recognized him. He knew he'd never seen the man before, but he recognized him from having heard his description, and he knew that Howard Clark was making his move tonight.

"But why have we come down here?" Lisa Lee asked Jonathan Biggs, frowning at the streets of the Barbary Coast as they passed them in their hired buggy.

"We are slumming tonight, my dear," Biggs said, smiling. "Portsmouth Square can get to be such a bore at times, don't you agree?"

"Perhaps," she said, "but never boring enough to warrant coming here."

"Don't tell me you've never been here before, Miss Lisa Lee," Biggs said, and his tone of voice made the Oriental girl look at him sharply.

"Not for a long time," she said slowly.

"Ah yes," Jonathan said, "you are above this now, aren't you?"

"I have gone past this, yes," she said. "I would prefer not to come back to the Barbary Coast or to Chinatown. Not willingly, anyway."

"Relax, my dear," Jonathan said. "You are not coming back to stay, only to visit."

"One is too close to the other for my comfort."

Jonathan Biggs laughed softly and closed one of his hands over one of her small ones.

"I shall protect you, have no fear."

Clint Adams watched the man he recognized as

Long Taylor—the man's long face was a very distinctive characteristic—as he finished his drink and ordered another. Taylor did not look at Clint Adams. In fact, he looked everywhere *but* at the Gunsmith, which was what made Clint Adams sure that the man was there for him.

Now that he knew what form Howard Clark's action was going to take, he was strangely calm about it. Knowing what was coming had that effect, because he knew that he was equipped to handle it. Whether or not he would come out ahead was a question that would soon be answered, but at least he knew he would be up to the challenge.

Clint looked away from Long Taylor just as the batwing doors opened and he saw Jonathan Biggs enter with Lisa Lee on his arm. The Oriental woman commanded the attention of every man in the place, all of whom studied her with blatant hunger in their eyes—Long Taylor no exception. In fact, he had a hungrier look than any other man in the place.

As Biggs and Lisa Lee crossed the room Jonathan spotted Clint, and grinning, propelled the Chinese girl toward his table.

"Mr. Archer, how delightful to see you."

"What the hell are you doing here?" Clint demanded. He was trying to look past Jonathan at Long Taylor, without seeming to.

"Sit down!" he said sharply, and Biggs first held a chair for Lisa Lee, and then sat down himself.

"Who can we give our order to?"

"If you want a drink in this place you better walk to the bar and get it."

"How quaint," Biggs said. He stood and walked to

the bar slowly, as if he were fascinated by having to do so.

"What the hell are *you* doing here?" Clint demanded of Lisa Lee.

"I did not know he wanted to come here, or I certainly would not have come. I also did not know you were here."

"Yeah, he didn't seem to know, either," Clint said, although he wondered.

Jonathan Biggs came back with a drink for himself and one for Lisa Lee.

"I'm afraid they didn't have any champagne, my dear," he said, putting a beer before her.

"This is fine."

Jonathan looked at Clint and said, "What a lively place this is."

"Not your kind of place."

"Quite the contrary. I like it very much. It's so colorful, if you know what I mean."

"Oh, I know what you mean, all right," Clint said, keeping a sharp eye on Long Taylor. He was about to look away when Taylor pushed away from the bar and started toward his table.

"Jonathan, if you're smart you'll take Lisa Lee and get her out of here."

"Is something exciting about to take place?" Jonathan Biggs asked eagerly. He turned in his seat to look behind him just as Long Taylor reached the table.

"How much you want for the chink girl?" Taylor asked.

"I beg your pardon?" Biggs said.

Taylor looked at Biggs, dismissed him, and looked at Clint.

"How much?"

"The lady is not for hire, Taylor."

Taylor's eyebrows went up in surprise and he said, "You know who I am? I'm flattered."

"What do you want?"

"I told you. I want to know how much—"

"Forget that horse manure, Taylor, and tell me what you really want."

When Taylor smiled, his face got longer and more unpleasant.

"I want you, Gunsmith, out in the street."

"It's dark out there."

"It's light enough for what we have to do."

Clint Adams was a man who avoided trouble when he could, but when he had decided to help Wing and Chang he'd known that trouble was inevitable, and that he'd have to handle it when it did finally rear its ugly head.

"Any way to avoid this?"

Taylor's smile widened and he said, "Nope." The only time Long Taylor ever really smiled was just before and just after he killed a man.

"All right."

"Just a moment," Jonathan Biggs said then, standing up. "The lady is with me," he said to Taylor. "If you have insulted her, then it is you and I who should step out into the street."

Taylor's dead eyes looked at Biggs, and then looked away.

"Pardon me," Biggs said, placing his hand on Taylor's chest.

"Are you wearing a gun?" Taylor asked.

"Why, no."

"You came down to the Barbary Coast without a gun?" Clint asked.

"I came here to gamble, not to kill anyone."

"And what do you intend to do with me once we get out into the street?" Taylor asked Biggs.

"Why, thrash you."

"With your fists?"

"That's right."

Taylor gave Clint a look that said, "Is he kidding?" and then he viciously backhanded Jonathan Biggs across the face. Biggs flew above the table and crashed down on top of it, shattering it beneath him.

"Outside," Taylor said to Clint.

"I'll be right there."

As Taylor headed for the door Howard Clark came out of his office to see what the commotion was. When he saw Biggs sprawled on the floor atop the pieces of the table he rushed over.

"I'm sorry—" he said, reaching down to help Biggs to his feet.

Biggs pushed him away angrily, then looked at Clint.

"Where did he go?"

"Outside. He's waiting for me."

"I will go—" Biggs said, staggering to his feet. Lisa Lee, who had never left her seat, stood up and put her hand on Biggs's arm.

"He'll kill you, Jonathan," she said. "Let Archer go."

"His name's not Archer," Howard Clark said. "It's Clint Adams."

Clint looked at Clark and said, "I'm going to go outside and take care of your man for you, Clark, and then I'm coming back in here to talk to you. I'd like to know how you know my real name."

"You'll never know, Adams," the saloon owner said, "because you're not coming back in."

"We'll see."

As he started for the doors he heard Clark speaking solicitously to Jonathan Biggs, and Biggs telling him to be quiet.

THIRTY-ONE

In all the years that the Gunsmith had been living by his gun, he could count on one hand the number of gunfights he'd had at night. The advantage was that you didn't have to worry about having the sun at your back. The disadvantage was obvious—if you had bad night-vision, you were in trouble. The fact that the darkness would force you to shoot at a closer distance could be called an advantage or a disadvantage. That depended on the individual. Some men liked to see their victim's eyes before they killed them. If there was fear there, it fueled their confidence. Others liked to watch their opponent's eyes because they tipped off their next move.

Clint Adams usually didn't have to worry about tip-offs because he was far faster than the men he'd had to face. Very few times—as with Kid Dragon and Bill Wallmann—was there even a hint of uncertainty about his ability to outdraw an opponent.

Long Taylor's reputation was well known, but Clint Adams had never seen the man's move, and it was dark out.

There was a hint of uncertainty, yes, but the Gunsmith had long ago decided that when his time came, it would be at the hands of a faster man, so he was prepared for it.

If this was the time, then so be it.

When he stepped out into the street he was gratified to see that most of the lamps were undamaged and lit. Long Taylor was standing in the center of the street, waiting, and a few people had stopped on the street to watch. From behind him he knew that people were leaving the saloon, also to watch. Were Chang and Wing among them? He didn't have time to dwell on that question.

"There's plenty of light," Long Taylor said from the street. Clint decided not to reply, and Taylor took the hint and remained silent.

The Gunsmith moved out into the center of the street and blocked out all of the spectators. Nothing existed beyond Long Taylor. Clint's eyes took in the entire man: his eyes, his shoulders, his gunhand. His upper body would give his move away. It would tense just moments before he drew.

Jonathan Biggs stepped out onto the boardwalk with Lisa Lee behind him, and Howard Clark stepped out behind her.

"What do you think?" Clark asked, eyeing the two men in the street.

Biggs threw Clark a look and didn't answer. Lisa Lee put her hand on Biggs's arm and squeezed. He could feel the tension in her body, and when he looked at her, her eyes were on the Gunsmith.

"This will be interesting."

Sam Wing, watching from the side, had no fear that Clint Adams would not be able to outdraw the other man.

But then, he had never heard of Long Taylor.

Long Taylor, who had always been satisfied with his reputation, knew that if he pulled this off, his notoriety would double. Not long ago the Gunsmith had killed Bill Wallmann, who some had thought was the fastest man alive with a gun since Hickok's death. Long Taylor, however, had always known that he was faster than Wallmann, and now he was about to prove that he was faster than the legendary Gunsmith—and would become a legend himself in the process.

The Gunsmith was surprised at how easily he picked up Taylor's move. When he drew, the gunman's hand was still moving toward his gun. After having faced Bill Wallmann, this was significantly easier.

He guessed that today was not the day, after all.

When the bullet struck him in the chest Long Taylor had only a moment to register disbelief before a black curtain fell over his eyes.

"Damn!" Howard Clark said under his breath and backed into the saloon.

Jonathan Biggs turned and looked after Howard Clark, then looked at Lisa Lee and said, "It's time for us to go, my dear. This place has ceased to be of interest."

THIRTY-THREE

Clint Adams quickly holstered his gun, and as a crowd formed around the fallen form of Long Taylor, he moved into the darkness of an alley and toward the back of the Black Pearl Saloon. His intention was to enter the saloon through the back door, but as he reached it he saw Howard Clark leaving. No doubt Clark remembered Clint's promise to come back and ask him a few questions after he was done with Taylor.

"Going somewhere?" he asked Clark.

The saloon owner turned quickly and stared into the darkness, trying to see who had spoken.

"I told you I'd come back to talk to you, Clark," Clint said, advancing on the man.

"Adams!"

"That's right."

Clint put his hand against Clark's chest and pushed him hard up against the building.

"Take it easy."

"It's time for us to stop playing games," Clint said. "I've been waiting for some sign that you're involved with the Black Pearl Tong, but since I don't believe in coincidence, and you picked the same name for your saloon—probably because you thought you were being clever—I'm going to ask you straight out."

"Ask me what?"

159

"Don't act stupid, Clark," the Gunsmith said, jabbing the man's breastbone hard with his forefinger. "You're involved with the tong, right?"

"I can't—I'll be killed—"

Clint rarely pulled his gun unless he was going to use it, but in this case he made an exception. He figured a point had to be made, and his gun would help him make it.

He drew his gun and pressed the still-hot barrel against the side of Clark's neck.

"I'll kill you right here and now if you don't answer me. You'd better believe it."

Clark's eyes were wide and sweat was rolling down his face. The smell of fear coming from him was acrid and unpleasant.

"Now," Clint said, jamming the barrel harder into the side of his neck.

"All right, all right," Clark said quickly. "I'm involved with the tong, but I ain't the leader."

"Now comes the big question," Clint said, increasing the pressure of the gun barrel again. "Who is?"

"You go out to the Biggs ranch and ask that question," Clark said.

"I'm asking *you*."

"And I just answered it," Clark said, his voice becoming firmer. "Now either you can go out to the Biggs ranch and ask it, or you can pull that trigger now."

"And what do you intend to do?"

"I intend to get the hell out of San Francisco as fast as I can," Clark explained, "because after the tong kills you, they'll come after me.'

"So you figure that while I keep them busy, you can make good your escape."

"That's right."

Clint stared into Clark's eyes for a few seconds, then took his gun away from his neck and holstered it.

"You better get moving, Clark."

"I'm on my way."

As Clark sprinted into the darkness, someone came up behind Clint. He reacted quickly and pointed his gun at Sam Wing's face.

"The Biggs ranch?" Sam Wing repeated.

"That's what the man said," Clint replied, putting his gun down. "Have you seen John?"

Wing looked embarrassed and said, "Uh, no."

"Maybe he's out at the Biggs ranch, then."

"No," a voice said from the darkness, "he isn't."

"John?" Wing said, peering into the shadows.

John Chang seemed to appear from nowhere, dressed all in black.

"What the hell have you been doing?" Sam Wing demanded.

"I've been following Clint for days, waiting for something to happen," John Chang said, "and now something has."

"Sam's been worried about you, John."

"Really?"

"No, I have not."

Chang looked at Wing, and then back to Clint.

"We can discuss this later," John Chang said. "It sounds to me like all our answers are out at the Biggs ranch."

"I agree," Sam Wing said.

"And maybe Su Chow," John added.

Clint and Sam Wing exchanged glances, but neither said what they were thinking.

"There's only one way to find out for sure," Clint

said, "so we'd better get going."

"Now? In the dark?" Sam Wing said.

"Did you see the man and the woman who were sitting with me?"

"Yes."

"That was Jonathan Biggs."

"And now he knows what happened here," Chang said.

"He's probably on his way back to the ranch right now," Clint said.

"Do you think he's the tong leader?" Sam Wing asked.

"I don't know," Clint said. "It's unlikely, but that could be an act. Again, there's only one way to find out, and that's to get out there *now*."

Wing and Chang exchanged looks, and then Chang said, "Let's go."

THIRTY-FOUR

"Why the hell didn't you kill him?" Frank Fletcher demanded of Jonathan Biggs. He was talking about Howard Clark.

"Are you forgetting who you're talking to, Fletcher?" Biggs replied calmly.

"No," Fletcher said, and then lowering his voice he said again, "No, I'm not forgetting, but it seems to me that if you knew he was going to talk you should have killed him."

"There were too many people around, and under the circumstances I thought I should get back here as soon as possible."

"Did you have to bring the girl?"

"Lisa Lee? I didn't have time to leave her off. Don't worry about her. As long as I pay her enough she won't get suspicious."

Lisa Lee was sitting in the living room with a cup of tea while Biggs and Fletcher were talking in Daniel Biggs's office.

"All right, then," Fletcher said. "If Clark talked, then that means we've got to get ready for some company."

"How many men do we have on the ground?"

"There are thirty men."

"How many of them are tong members?"

163

"More than half."

"All right. Dismiss the ones that aren't."

"What do I tell them?"

"Tell them to go into town and have a good time," Biggs said. "Use your imagination, Frank."

"What if some of them don't want to go?"

"Then fire the bastards and tell them to get their asses off my land!"

"You mean your father's land."

"Fletcher, I think I'm going to have to reevaluate your importance to the tong."

"All right, all right," Fletcher said. "I'm going."

"Get them out of here as soon as possible. When Adams and those two chink detectives get here I don't want anyone on the grounds but tong people."

"And the girl?"

"I'll take care of the girl, Fletcher," Biggs said testily. "You just do your part."

"I always do my part."

Fletcher left, glad that hard times had fallen on Howard Clark. Now perhaps he'd be able to take his rightful place as right-hand man to the tong leader. All they had to do was take care of the Gunsmith and those two detectives. They had more than enough men for that.

Jonathan Biggs moved to the window of his father's office and watched Frank Fletcher hurry to the bunkhouse. He turned then and removed the Winchester '73 from its place on the wall above the fireplace. He then moved to the desk, put the rifle on top, opened the bottom drawer, drew out a holster and gun, and strapped it on. He checked the action on both weapons and then carefully loaded them.

He was sorry that he hadn't had time to stop and leave Lisa Lee off. Now he was afraid that she might have to become tong property, and she was just independent—and determined—enough to want to fight that decision.

Jonathan hoped that he could convince her to cooperate, because if she remained stubborn, it would be too bad for her.

THIRTY-FIVE

Clint and the two Oriental detectives pulled their horses to a stop some distance from the Biggs ranch and dismounted.

"We'd do better to go the rest of the way on foot," Clint said.

"What's the difference?" an impatient John Chang asked. "They know we're coming."

"They don't know exactly when though," Clint said. "Let's get in there as quietly as possible and we may be able to avoid a lot of bloodshed."

"I won't mind a little bloodshed," John Chang said with feeling, and Wing looked toward Clint and shook his head to indicate that his partner was still not himself.

They started for the Biggs ranch on foot, moving as swiftly and quietly as they could.

"How many do you think we will have to face?" Sam Wing asked.

"A ranch this size has to have a lot of men. I'm hoping we'll be able to bypass most of them. The only man I want to deal with is the tong leader."

"I'm afraid John feels the same way, although he wouldn't mind going through a few men to get to him."

"I just hope he won't shoot until we have to. There's no sense in advertising our arrival."

"What the hell—" Sam Wing said as they came within sight of the ranch house.

"Quiet," Clint said.

The area of the house was lit up and, from what they could see, a good portion of the men who probably worked there were mounted up and leaving. In the center of all the activity was Frank Fletcher.

"What are they doing, pulling out?" John Chang asked, sounding puzzled.

"There's only one thing I can figure," Clint Adams said.

"What's that?"

"All of the men who work here probably are not members of the tong."

"So they're getting rid of the ones who aren't," Chang finished.

"That's the only explanation I can think of."

"It looks like quite a few of them are leaving," Sam Wing observed.

"I'm sure there are plenty of them left," Clint said. "Come on, let's try to use the confusion to work our way around the back. Maybe we can get in that way."

They circled the point of all the activity and eventually found themselves behind the house, where there was considerably less going on.

"Before we do anything we've got to search the house," John Chang said. "Su Chow has to be inside."

"Unless she's in the barn," Sam Wing added.

Chang looked at Wing to see if his partner was serious, and then decided himself that taking a look in the barn might be the wise thing to do.

"I'll look."

"Go through the back of the barn, John," Clint said, advising him. "We'll wait here. The three of us would be·easier to spot."

"I'll be back."

They watched as John Chang moved toward the rear door of the barn and tried the door. He opened it and disappeared inside.

"She's dead," Sam Wing said when his friend was out of sight. "She's got to be."

"I agree."

They didn't say anything more after that and simply watched the rear of the barn, waiting for John Chang to reappear.

"There he is," Sam Wing said.

"From the look on his face I'd say there was nothing in the barn but horses."

Which was, of course, no surprise to either of them.

"Empty," John Chang said.

"Too bad," his partner said.

"All right, let's move toward the house," the Gunsmith said. "It's time to get this over with."

THIRTY-SIX

Moving one by one, they successfully made it to the rear of the house without raising an alarm. The night was quiet, and from the sounds they could hear from the front of the house, the exodus of men was still going on.

"I think by leaving right away we made it a little earlier than they had anticipated," Clint said. "We might get through this thing without having to tangle with the men that are left."

"Let's get inside," John Chang said impatiently.

Wing put his hand on Chang's arm and said, "Take it easy, John."

"Don't worry," his partner said, "I'm not going to overreact and start shooting."

"That's good to hear," Clint said. "Come on."

He tried the rear door and found it locked.

"Let me," Wing said, producing a knife. Clint stepped aside and Wing used the knife to force the door open quietly.

"All right," he said, pocketing the knife. He opened the door wide and stepped in, followed by Clint and John Chang.

They were in a hallway and, following it, found themselves in the kitchen.

"Listen," Clint whispered.

They all stood still and could hear the low hum of voices in steady conversation.

Clint waved his hand for the other two to follow and moved toward the kitchen entrance. From there it was apparent to him that the conversation was taking place in the old man's office.

"One of us should check out the upstairs," he whispered.

"I will," Chang offered.

"Be careful," Sam Wing warned him.

"If you find anyone up there besides Su Chow you're going to have to immobilize them."

"Don't worry," Chang said, "I will." The look in his eye told Clint how.

"You'll have to do it quietly, too."

"I will."

"All right, then. Go ahead."

Chang moved to the doorway, peered out, then left the relative safety of the kitchen and moved toward the stairway. If anyone came out of the office at that moment Chang would be in plain sight, but he made it to the steps without that happening. While Chang was on the steps, however, the front door began to open and both Clint and Sam Wing caught their breath. They couldn't see John Chang from their vantage point and could only hope that he was out of sight.

The man who entered by the front door *was* in their line of sight, however; it was Frank Fletcher. He entered and without a wayward glance made his way directly to the door of the office.

"Fletcher," a voice said from inside when he opened the door, but the rest of what was said was cut off when the man with the patch closed the door behind him. From the single word, however, Clint felt sure that the speaker was Jonathan Biggs.

"That was close," Sam Wing said.

Clint nodded.

"When John comes back down we're going to have to go into that office. Once we get the drop on them the men outside won't be able to help them."

"Right," Wing said. "All we've got to do is wait for John to come back down."

But waiting was a lot harder to do than it sounded.

When Frank entered the office Jonathan Biggs looked up and said, "Fletcher—how's it going?"

"All of the men who aren't with us are off the grounds," Fletcher replied. "The others are deployed all around the house. They won't be able to get in."

"Fine," the other man in the room said. He was sitting behind the desk, a situation which clearly did not please Jonathan Biggs. "Perhaps we might still ride out the results of your incompetence," the man said, directing his remark at Jonathan.

"Now wait just a minute—"

"No, we don't have a minute to wait and soothe your wounded pride," the man behind the desk said. "For all we know, Adams and those two Oriental detectives may already be inside the house."

"That's ridiculous."

"Is it?" The other man looked past Jonathan Biggs at Frank Fletcher and asked, "Has the house been checked?"

"No."

"Then check it. Start with the upstairs. You might get another man to help you."

Fletcher looked at Jonathan Biggs, the implied question being why couldn't *he* help, but the seated man said, "Jonathan and I have some other things to discuss."

"All right."

"Do it as quickly as you can and report back."

"Right."

Fletcher left the room hoping that the old man was going to peel the hide off of Biggs.

Upstairs John Chang's heart was pounding as he moved along a hallway, checking out all of the rooms on the second floor. At each door he held his breath and opened it, gun ready, hoping to find Su Chow, possibly bound and gagged, but healthy and alive.

Actually, his heart was still pounding from having been trapped on the steps when Fletcher entered the house. Chang had simply frozen, hoping that Fletcher would not look up the steps. When he had moved unerringly toward the door of the office, Chang had breathed a momentary sigh of relief.

Now he was holding his breath again, standing at the last door to be checked. He cocked the hammer on his gun, then turned the knob and thrust the door open.

"Yes," he whispered as he saw, lying on a bed, the small figure of a woman, bound and gagged—but definitely alive!

Clint and Sam Wing had been about to vacate the kitchen and move toward the office when once again the door opened and Fletcher stepped out.

"Now what?" Clint whispered.

Fletcher moved toward the front door, opened it, and shouted to someone to come up to the house.

Turning to face Wing, Clint said, "I think he's calling for help to search the house."

"Let him. We will be waiting for them."

"What about John? He's upstairs, he doesn't know—"

"John will take care of himself, Clint," Sam Wing said. "I suggest that we do the same."

A man joined Fletcher at the front door, and they could hear the foreman giving him instructions to thoroughly search the upstairs while he did the same down here.

"All right," Clint said, "let's back up and find a good place to wait for him. This might work in our favor."

"I hope so."

Clint only hoped that John Chang wouldn't end up being surprised upstairs. Silence was the most important key to their success. If the rest of the men on the ranch became aware of their presence, their chances of getting out alive would be almost nil.

THIRTY-SEVEN

The girl's eyes followed John Chang's progress into the room. She didn't know who he was, so she couldn't know whether or not she should have been afraid of him.

"Su Chow," he said to her. She wanted to tell him she wasn't Su Chow, but the gag kept her from doing that.

The Chinese man holstered his gun and moved toward the bed, falling down onto one knee.

"Su Chow, I've found you," he said, hurriedly untying her hands. When her hands were free she pulled the gag away from her mouth so she could speak.

"Who are you?" she demanded. "What's going on?"

All she knew was that, after she had refused to go along with Jonathan's plans for her—to make her the property of some tong—he'd had the horrible man with the patch take her up here and tie her up.

"Su Chow—" the man said, again, but he was frowning and this time it came out a question.

"My name is not Su Chow," she said. "It's Lisa Lee. My name is Lisa Lee."

"Lisa—you're not Su Chow."

"No."

The pained look on the man's face made her feel sorry for him. Whoever this Su Chow was he obviously loved her very much.

"I'm sorry," she said.

He looked directly at her, and suddenly his face changed. It became impassive, totally devoid of any expression.

"Come on, get up," he said. "We have to get you out of here."

Lisa Lee stood up and momentarily leaned on the man.

"Are you all right?" he asked.

"Yes, yes," she said, pushing away from him. "I'm all right now."

"Then let's go."

He moved toward the door with Lisa Lee in tow. As he reached it, he became aware that there was someone in the hallway.

"Who—" she started to say, but he put a hand up to stop her.

"Someone is in the hall?" he whispered.

"What do we do?"

"We wait," he said, "to see who they are, and how many. Don't worry, we'll get out of here."

Clint and Sam Wing backed into the kitchen, moved to opposite sides, and waited for Frank Fletcher to make his appearance. They were going to try to take him quietly, without killing him.

Fletcher was checking every other room on the first floor before the kitchen. But eventually they heard him walking down the hall toward them.

"Get ready," Clint mouthed at Sam Wing.

As Fletcher entered they moved fast. Wing came up

behind him and stuck his gun in his back, while Clint moved in front of him and pulled Fletcher's gun from his holster.

"Hello, Fletcher," he said.

The man's lone eye stared angrily at him, and his mouth drew down at the corners. He knew better than to say anything, though. He knew he was potentially moments away from death.

"Smart man," Clint said to Wing. "He knows when to keep quiet." Clint looked at Fletcher and said, "Now we're going to go and see your boss. Let's go, down the hall."

Wing moved aside to allow Fletcher to turn around, and then he and Clint walked behind him until they reached the door to the office.

"Open it," Clint instructed him.

Fletcher hesitated, but Wing increased the pressure of his gun against the man's back, so he turned the doorknob and pushed the door open.

"Fletcher—" Jonathan Biggs said, and then saw the two men behind him.

"Don't try it," Clint called out as Biggs started to reach for the rifle reclining against the desk. The old man behind the desk made no move toward a weapon.

"Don't," the old man told Jonathan Biggs.

"But father," Jonathan said to Daniel Biggs, the leader of the Black Pearl Tong.

"Never mind, Jonathan." Daniel Biggs turned his head toward the door and said to Clint, "Come in Mr. Adams. We've been expecting you, although, I might add, not so soon."

"I'm sorry to disappoint you," Clint said, pushing Fletcher into the room ahead of them.

"You have discovered our secret, I assume."

"From what I can tell, you and your son actually run the tong together."

"Hah," Frank Fletcher said, and Jonathan Biggs threw him a dirty look.

"Mr. Fletcher has his opinions about Jonathan, I'm afraid, as I do, but yes, basically you are correct."

"It's over now, though."

"Perhaps," Daniel Biggs said. "I have a lot of men outside this house."

"That's just the point, Mr. Biggs. They're outside and we're in here."

"You've got to go out sometimes, though."

"Yes," Clint said, pushing Fletcher away from them, "but you'll go with us."

"That won't matter," Biggs said. "My men have strict orders not to let anyone on or off the grounds, no matter what."

"They won't shoot while we have you."

The senior Biggs looked staight into the Gunsmith's eyes and said, "On their lives, they'd better."

THIRTY-EIGHT

Clint believed him, which meant they were at something of an impasse.

"What would you like to do now, Mr. Adams?" Daniel Biggs asked.

"I'd like to get the hell out of here."

"Go ahead."

"It's not that easy."

"Do you have someone else in the house?"

"No."

"Where's the other one?" Jonathan Biggs asked. "The other chink detective?"

"He's been missing."

"You expect us to believe that?"

"He's probably upstairs," Daniel Biggs said. "Did you send a man upstairs, Fletcher?"

"Yes, sir."

Clint and Sam Wing exchanged glances, and Wing nodded, indicating that his partner could take care of himself.

"Whatever is happening upstairs shouldn't concern you, Mr. Biggs," Clint said. "Your Black Pearl Tong is finished."

"I think not."

The man's confidence was disturbing, especially

181

since he was displaying it so prominently while under the gun.

"My advice to you, Mr. Adams, would be to give up your guns. I will make sure that your deaths are quick and painless."

"What happened to the girl?" Sam Wing asked. "What happened to Su Chow?"

"Su Chow?" Biggs said, looking at his son. "What's he talking about."

"Just a girl. She wasn't important."

"What happened to her?"

"Nothing."

"Jonathan—"

"He killed her," Frank Fletcher said.

"Shut up!" Jonathan hissed.

"She's the reason I'm here," Clint said, "and the reason Sam Wing and his partner got involved."

"A girl, a Chinese girl?"

"Yes."

Biggs threw his son a disgusted look.

"One of your whores?"

"She wasn't a whore!" John Chang shouted from behind them and charged into the room.

Empty-handed John Chang charged Jonathan Biggs, grabbing him around the throat. As he did so Frank Fletcher moved, tackling Sam Wing around the waist. The two men went tumbling to the floor, and Daniel Biggs rose from his desk and reached for the Winchester leaning against the desk.

"Don't," Clint warned.

The old man looked at Clint and actually smiled.

"If it is to end, then let it end," he said. He reached for the rifle and picked it up.

"Mr. Biggs—"

Biggs jacked a round into the chamber and started to bring the rifle to bear on Clint Adams.

"Damn it, then let it end," the Gunsmith said, and fired one round into Daniel Biggs's chest.

THIRTY-NINE

"How's John?"

"He's all right," Sam Wing said. "The worst part of all was not knowing what happened to her." Wing shrugged and said, "Now he knows."

They were meeting in the detectives' office for the last time. When Clint left there, he was also leaving San Francisco. He'd had quite enough of that city for a while.

After Clint had shot Daniel Biggs, Sam Wing had no problem taking care of Frank Fletcher, but he hadn't been in time to keep his partner from killing Jonathan Biggs. After that, they had heard shooting from outside, and later discovered that Inspector Kovac and his men had shown up at the ranch. Kovac had responded to the shoot-out in front of the Black Pearl Saloon, and later had picked up Howard Clark trying to leave the city. He had told the policeman to go to the Biggs ranch.

"Lucky for us Kovac showed up," Clint said now, "or we'd still be trying to shoot our way out."

"Or we'd be dead."

Clint nodded.

"I guess our friend the Inspector will be glad to see you go," Sam Wing said.

"Yeah, but he still has you two to put up with. Why

don't you give him a break and wait a month or so before you break another tong."

"There's one thing I still don't know."

"What's that?"

"What was Madame Pearl's connection with this?"

"Nothing major," Clint said. "I spoke to her earlier. The tong backed her place, and she entertained people for Biggs whenever he sent them over."

"She didn't supply them with girls for slave trade or anything?"

"She says not, and Kovac can't prove she did, so she's still in business."

"Perhaps I should take John there," Sam Wing said. "There is nothing like a woman to help a man *forget* a woman."

"Ask for Little Chrissie," Clint said, standing up, "or why don't you simply get him Lisa Lee?"

"I might do both," Sam Wing said, also standing. He extended his hand toward the Gunsmith and said, "Thank you for all your help, my friend."

"I've got the hardest job coming up," Clint said, pumping the detective's hand.

"What's that?"

"I've got to get in touch with Dan Chow and tell him that his sister was dead before I got here."

"Good luck."

"Thanks," the Gunsmith said. "I'll need it."